P9-ARQ-374

GREAT ILLUSTRATED CLASSICS

JANE EYRE

Charlotte Bronte

Adapted by
Malvina G. Vogel

Illustrations by Pablo Marcos

South Huntington Pub. Lib.
145 Pidgeon Hill Rd.
Huntington Sta., N.Y. 11746

ABDO
Publishing Company

J. Bronte

GREAT ILLUSTRATED CLASSICS

edited by
Rochelle Larkin

visit us at
www.abdopub.com

Library edition published in 2005 by ABDO Publishing Company, 4940 Viking Drive, Suite 622, Edina, Minnesota 55435. Published by agreement with Playmore Incorporated Publishers and Waldman Publishing Corporation.

Cover art, interior art, and text copyright © 1990 by Playmore Incorporated Publishers and Waldman Publishing Corporation, New York, New York.

International copyrights reserved in all countries. No part of this book may be reproduced in any form without written permission from the publisher.

Printed in the United States.

Library of Congress Cataloging-in-Publication Data

Vogel, Malvina G.
    Jane Eyre / Charlotte Bronte ; adapted by Malvina G. Vogel ; illustrations by Pablo Marcos ; edited by Rochelle Larkin.
        p. cm. -- (Great illustrated classics)
    Summary: An abridged version of the story of an orphaned young English woman who accepts employment as a governess at Thornfield Hall, a country estate owned by the mysteriously remote Mr. Rochester.
    ISBN 1-59679-243-4
    [1. Orphans--Fiction. 2. Governesses--Fiction. 3. Great Britain--History--19th century--Fiction.] I. Brontë, Charlotte, 1816-1855. Jane Eyre. II. Larkin, Rochelle. III. Marcos, Pablo, ill. IV. Title. V. Series.

PZ7.V86723Jan 2005
[Fic]--dc22

                                                                        2004062307

Contents

About the Author

Charlotte Bronte was born in 1816. She was one of six children of a poor country preacher. Her mother died when she was only five. Charlotte and her sisters attended Cowan Bridge, a school for clergymen's children. Many readers wonder whether that school was the model for the Lowood School in *Jane Eyre*. Sadly, it was the school where Charlotte's two older sisters died of tuberculosis. Charlotte and her other sisters returned home for safekeeping themselves and were taught by their aunt.

At home, Charlotte, her brother Branwell, and her sisters wrote fantasy stories to entertain themselves. The world of make-believe became very important to all of them. She later attended a better school, where she became a teacher, then held two brief but dull positions as governess to wealthy families.

Charlotte's love of writing continued from her teen years into her twenties and thirties. She published her first novel, *Jane Eyre*, in 1847. It was an instant success. But it wasn't published under her own name. Its author was identified as Currer Bell. Charlotte probably chose to use a man's name for several reasons: first, because there was prejudice against women novelists in the nineteenth century, and second, because she didn't want to embarrass friends who might recognize themselves in her novel.

Charlotte Bronte was dedicated to her writing and didn't marry until she was thirty-eight years old. Sadly, after less than a year of marriage, and pregnant with her first child, she died of tuberculosis in 1855.

They Made My Life Miserable.

CHAPTER 1

My Sad Early Life

I was an orphan and nobody ever let me forget it. My parents had died when I was just an infant, and my mother's brother, Uncle Reed, took me in to live with his family at their estate, Gateshead. He was kind to me, but when I was three, he died too. His wife, Aunt Reed, and their three children turned against me and made my life miserable.

My cousins, John, Eliza and Georgiana, blamed me for things I didn't do and told lies to their mother about me. When I tried to defend myself to Aunt Reed, she would never believe me and would order me out of her sight. She would punish me by not letting anyone talk to me for hours and sometimes even days.

So, I would often go off by myself to read in my own private world, a window seat with heavy drapes that I could wrap around myself and hide in. Here, I would escape… that is, until fourteen-year-old John would decide to look for me. He always managed to find me.

John spent a great deal of time at home rather than at school because, his mama said, he was in poor health. But it was because he ate too much candy and cake, which showed in his pimply face and many chins.

The worst time I can remember is the day I was reading on my window seat and he stormed into the room, shouting, "Come here!"

I obeyed, because I knew I had to. He then spent three minutes sticking his tongue out at me until I thought it would tear off from its roots. Then he suddenly smacked my face with all his strength.

My Own Private World

I fell back from his blow, but managed to stay on my feet. "I was only reading my book, Master John," I said, trying my best not to cry.

"That is not your book," he snapped. "You own nothing in his house, no books, no clothes, no toys, nothing! You don't even have the right to eat the same food as we do or sleep in the nursery with us. We are children of a lady and a gentleman, and you have no father or mother."

With that, he grabbed the book from my hands and flung it at my head. I fell against a table, cutting open my head as I went down. As the blood began dripping from the wound, my terror disappeared and anger took its place.

"Wicked, cruel boy!" I cried. "You are an evil tyrant, like the Roman slave drivers!"

"How dare you speak to me like that!" he shouted, grabbing my hair.

I remember swinging my arms furiously, but whether or not I hit him, I don't recall.

While this was happening, Eliza and Georgiana ran for their mother, but Bessie, the housemaid who had always been kind to me, reached us first.

Before I had a chance to explain, Aunt Reed burst into the room. "Take her away!" she ordered Bessie, "and lock her in the red room."

I fought all the way as I was being dragged upstairs. Fighting back was a new response for me. Usually, I gave in and kept quiet.

"Jane, Jane, shame on you," Bessie scolded. "How could you strike your young master?"

"He is not my master," I shouted, "and I am not his servant or anyone else's."

"No, child," Bessie said gently, "but sadly, you are less than a servant, since you do nothing to earn your place here. You are entirely dependent on Mrs. Reed's generosity." As she lifted me onto a stool in the red room, she spoke firmly. "Now sit here, and think over your wicked behavior."

But I wasn't about to sit. I jumped off and tried to run.

"Jane, if you don't stay still, I shall have to tie you down." And while she held me down with one hand, she started to pull off a band

"You Don't Have to Tie Me Down."

from her stocking with the other.

This took some of the fight out of me. "All right," I told her, "I'll sit still. You don't have to tie me down."

"You've never behaved like this before, Jane," Bessie said when she saw I was sitting quietly. "Whatever came over you? You must be grateful to the Reeds. If Mrs. Reed threw you out, you'd have to go to the poorhouse with other orphans and homeless people. You must try to be obedient, and make them like you."

Once Bessie had left and locked the door, I looked around this room. I had often been sent here as a punishment. It was a bedroom, but no one had slept in it or lit a fire in it since my Uncle Reed had died in it seven years before.

But in spite of what Bessie had said, I did not think about how to make the Reeds like me.

Reader, please believe that I had always tried to obey Aunt Reed, but she always blamed me for things I hadn't done. Nobody punished John for hitting me, but because I tried to defend myself, I was the one punished.

"It's not fair!" I cried to the empty room. "Should I run away or just stay here and starve myself and die?"

I realized that I was a nobody at Gateshead Hall. I was a hated intruder. Aunt Reed had promised her dying husband to raise me as one of her own children, but even though she kept me at Gateshead, which she hated doing, she never treated me as one of her own. I was certain that if Uncle Reed were alive, he would have been kinder to me.

With no fire in the red room and a heavy rain beating against the windows, the room got colder as it got darker. I shivered in my thin dress and looked over to the bed for something warm to wrap around me. But then I thought I heard a faraway voice. Was it Uncle Reed's? Was he talking to me?

"His ghost is here!" I cried in a panic, jumping down from the stool and running to the door. "The ghost! There's a ghost in here! It's Uncle Reed's ghost!"

Footsteps came running down the hall.

I Thought I Heard a Faraway Voice.

The door was unlocked and flung open. "What is all this?" Aunt Reed demanded.

"Please let me out! Please!" I cried. "I saw a ghost. It was Uncle Reed's ghost."

"You won't get out of here by lying and trying to trick me," she snapped.

"I shall die if I have to stay here!" I pleaded. "Punish me some other way. Have pity!"

"Be quiet! You know I can't stand hysterics. You are a clever little actress, but you can't fool me." And she pushed me back into the room, then closed and locked the door behind her.

I felt myself falling to the floor. Then darkness filled the world around me. I had fainted.

The next thing I remember was waking up in my own bed. Someone was lifting me up and resting my head against a pillow. I saw Mr. Lloyd, the town pharmacist, sitting beside my bed, with Bessie standing behind him.

If Aunt Reed or her children were sick, she would call a doctor, but for the servants or for me, she would only call the local pharmacist.

"Oh, Mr. Lloyd," I said weakly. "Am I very ill?"

"No, my child, you will be well soon," he said, smiling and patting my head. "I've given Bessie instructions for your care and I shall come by to see you again tomorrow."

After Mr. Lloyd left, my heart sank. Bessie leaned over me and asked, "Would you like something to eat or drink, Miss Jane?"

"No, thank you, Bessie," I answered, still frightened. But I did feel bold enough to ask, "What's the matter with me, Bessie? Am I ill?"

"No child, you just got sick from being in the red room and crying so much. Just try to sleep. I'm sure you'll be fine when you wake up tomorrow."

But I couldn't sleep. I still thought of the ghost of Uncle Reed in the red room, and those fears kept me awake, as they would keep most children awake.

The next day, I did feel a bit better, so Bessie wrapped me in a shawl and let me sit near the fireplace in the nursery. It was a peaceful day because all the Reeds had gone out to visit friends.

Bessie Brought Me Some Cookies.

Bessie brought me some cookies, though I didn't feel much like eating. I asked for my favorite book, *Gulliver's Travels*. But even with that book in my hands and with Bessie singing to me as she dusted the nursery, tears kept trickling down my cheeks.

Mr. Lloyd came again that day just as he had said he would. Even though Bessie told him I was doing well, he saw my wet eyes and cheeks.

"So you've been crying, Jane," he said. "Can you tell me why? Are you in pain?"

"N-n-no, s-sir," I sobbed.

Bessie then offered her reason for my tears. "Perhaps because she couldn't go out visiting with the family."

"Not at all!" I protested. "I wouldn't cry over that. I'm crying because I'm miserable."

"Miserable, Jane? Why?" Mr. Lloyd asked.

"Well, sir, she fell yesterday," Bessie said.

"I didn't fall," I insisted. "John pushed me down and smashed a book into my head, then my aunt locked me in the red room. But even that didn't make me ill, sir."

Then turning to Bessie, Mr. Lloyd said, "I'd like to speak to Miss Jane alone. Would you kindly leave us?"

With Bessie gone, Mr. Lloyd turned to me and asked, "If the fall didn't make you ill, what did?"

"I was locked up in the room where my uncle died. It was dark and cold, and I saw his ghost and thought he spoke to me. If I had anywhere else to go or any family to go to, I'd be glad to leave here. But I'm forced to stay here until I'm grown."

"Don't you have any relatives besides the Reeds?"

"I don't think so. I once asked Aunt Reed if I did and she said I might have some relatives named Eyre on my father's side, 'beggars,' she called them. But if they really did exist, she didn't know anything about them."

My tears had stopped and I went on. "They said my father was a poor clergyman and my mother's wealthy family were all so against her marrying him that they disowned her and left

"I'd Like to Speak to Miss Jane."

all their money to their son, Uncle Reed. And when my parents died from a terrible disease called typhus, my uncle took me in to raise me."

"Do you think you would like to go away to school instead of living here, Jane?" the kind pharmacist asked.

"I don't know, sir. John Reed says he hates his school, but Bessie always tells me that at school, girls can learn to read and paint and play music and sew and speak French. That does sound like things I would like to do."

"Well, perhaps some changes will come about in your life, Jane," said Mr. Lloyd as he got up to leave. "I hear Mrs. Reed's carriage returning and I have to speak to her for a moment." "Good-bye, Jane."

I later learned that Mr. Lloyd suggested to my aunt that she send me away to school. Aunt Reed was very happy at the idea of getting rid of me.

For the next several weeks, I was ignored completely by all the Reeds. Aunt Reed moved my bed into a tiny closet, away from the nursery where I had slept with her children, and she even made me eat all my meals alone.

For the next few months, including Christmas and New Year's, my life was the same awful existence. While for the others, there were parties and presents and dressing up in new clothes, I was left out of everything. But I didn't really mind being alone. I had my one doll and she spent every moment with me. I loved her because every human being must love something, and I treated her as if she were alive. Otherwise, I had no one.

"Don't Ask Questions. Just Go."

CHAPTER 2

Good-bye to Gateshead

It wasn't until the middle of January that things changed. One morning, Bessie came into the nursery where I was picking up the toys and dirty clothes that the Reed children had left lying around.

"Miss Jane, Mrs. Reed wants you downstairs in the breakfast room this very minute."

"But Aunt Reed hasn't spoken to me in three months. What does she want me for now?"

"Don't ask questions, child. Just go."

I felt myself trembling with fear as I started down the staircase. What are they going to punish me for now? I asked myself.

As I opened the door, I saw Aunt Reed in her usual chair at the fireside. Standing before her was a tall, thin man dressed all in black. He had a face as cold and as frightening as a stone mask.

"This is the girl I have spoken to you about," said Aunt Reed, pointing to me. "This is Jane Eyre."

"But you said she was ten years old, madam," said the man's cold voice. "She is so small for her age." Then he turned to me. "Are you a good child, Jane?" But he didn't ask it kindly.

Before I could answer, Aunt Reed shook her head and said, "We cannot discuss that now, Mr. Brocklehurst."

The man sat down and motioned for me to stand in front of him. "If your aunt won't discuss this, then you must be a naughty child. And do you know where naughty children go when they die?"

"They go to hell, sir."

"And how can you avoid that?"

"To avoid going to hell, sir, I must stay healthy and not die."

Cold as a Stone Mask

"That is a wicked answer from a wicked child!" he snarled.

A satisfied smile crossed Aunt Reed's face. "That is what I told you in my letter, Mr. Brocklehurst. If you accept her into Lowood School, everyone must be warned that she is a liar and a troublemaker."

I stood listening to her making my future life as miserable as she had made my past. But she wasn't finished.

"And also, Mr. Brocklehurst, on vacations, she is to stay at Lowood. I do not wish her to return here. At last, I will be free of the burden of raising her, for it is too much for me to bear!" And with a false gesture, she clutched at her heart.

As Mr. Brocklehurst got up to leave, he handed me a book. "Read this carefully, Jane. It is about a naughty girl like you who always told lies and how she died suddenly."

I stood in front of Aunt Reed after he left. She didn't even look at me. After a few minutes, she yelled, "Get out of the room!"

I started to go, then stopped at the door and

turned to her. "I am not a liar. If I were, I would say I loved you, but the truth is I don't love you. I hate you the worst of anyone in the world, except maybe your son John. And this book about liars should be given to John and to your daughters. They are the ones who tell lies, not I!"

Aunt Reed's hand froze in mid-air. "Are you quite finished?"

As I shook with rage, I shouted, "No, I'm not! I'm glad you are not related to me. I will never call you aunt again as long as I live. You've been cruel to me and made my life miserable. The thought of you makes me sick!"

"How dare you!" she thundered.

"How dare I? Because it is the truth. You think I have no feelings, that I don't need love and kindness? Until my dying day I shall never forget how you locked me in the red room and ignored me when I pleaded for help. People may think you're a good woman for taking me in, but you aren't. You're evil. You are the one who is full of lies and deceit."

Even though I was only ten years old, reader,

I Suddenly Felt Free.

I remember suddenly feeling free. I had spoken the truth and I knew I had won. For the first time in my life, I saw a look of fear come over Aunt Reed's face. She jumped out of her chair and rushed from the room.

Two days later, at five o'clock in the morning, I was dressed and ready to leave Gateshead.

Bessie came in to beg me to eat before I left, but I was too excited at the thought of my journey to put any food into my mouth. So she wrapped up some biscuits and put them into my bag.

"Are you glad to be leaving here, child?" she asked. "Glad to be leaving your poor Bessie?"

"I'm glad to be leaving Gateshead, but why should you care? You're always scolding me."

"Only to make you stronger and bolder, Jane."

"So I'd get more punishment?" I cried. But then I regretted my outburst. "I'm sorry, Bessie, you have been nice. I've liked you the best of anyone here."

I stood waiting at the gate, with Bessie beside me, as the coach pulled to a stop.

"Are you traveling alone, child?" asked the coachman as he lifted up my trunk. "It's a long way to Lowood, you know, fifty miles."

I nodded and smiled. "I want to be as far away from Gateshead and as far away from the Reeds as I can. Good-bye to all of them!" I shouted as I covered Bessie's pretty face with kisses. Then I climbed aboard.

The trip lasted all day and well into the rainy, windy night, with no moon to light our way.

When the coach finally stopped, I woke from a short sleep. The coach door opened and a young woman looked in at the passengers.

"Is there a girl named Jane Eyre here?" she asked.

I answered yes, and she lifted me out. My trunk was handed down and the coach rode off.

"I'm Miss Miller, Jane. I'm a teacher's helper," she explained. "It's only a short walk to the school. I'll send someone down for your trunk."

"It's a Long Way to Lowood."

I followed her into a big dark building. The room we entered was large, with long tables set up in rows. Seated at the tables, even at this time of night, were girls of every age between nine and twenty. There were at least eighty girls, all dressed in long dresses and white aprons.

"This is study hour," explained Miss Miller. Then she spoke loudly, giving orders to some of the older girls. "Monitors, bring in supper."

Supper was an oatcake and a mug of water. I was much too tired to eat, but I did want the water.

After supper, prayers were said. Then the girls went upstairs into long bedrooms with rows of small narrow beds. Two girls shared each bed.

A loud bell woke us while it was still so dark, I thought it was the middle of the night. The room was bitter cold and I shivered as I dressed, then waited my turn at the washbasin, which was shared by six girls.

We went down to the schoolroom, said our

morning prayers, and formed into four classes according to age. Each class was grouped around a center chair. I was given a place in the circle of the smallest children.

Soon, three women came in along with Miss Miller and took their seats. We read the Bible for the first hour, and by then it was daylight. I soon realized how hungry I was, since I hadn't eaten anything the day before.

As the monitors entered with the breakfast trays, I heard some of the girls grumble.

"Disgusting!" "Terrible!" "The porridge is burnt again!"

I was so hungry I gulped down the first two spoonfuls. But as soon as the hunger pains stopped, I suddenly felt nauseous.

Other girls tried to swallow their porridge, but gave up as well.

We had to say a prayer of thanks for food no one had been able to eat! Even the teachers whispered to each other about the food. "What horrible stuff!" "How shameful!"

When the clock struck nine, all the girls

"How Shameful!"

and their teachers took their seats silently.

Then everyone jumped to their feet, and just as quickly sat back down. I followed everyone's eyes to see why this was done, since I did not hear any orders given. Everyone sat staring at the woman who entered the room.

"Who is that?" I whispered to the girl beside me.

"That's Miss Temple," the girl whispered back with a smile. A toss of red curls peeked out from under her cap. "She's the Superintendent of Lowood and really nice."

Miss Temple took the oldest girls through their lessons in geography, using a globe on the table in front of her. The other teachers gave lessons in history, grammar, and arithmetic, with music lessons for the older girls.

Later, when the lunch bell rang, Miss Temple stood up and spoke to the entire group. "Since none of you could eat this morning's breakfast, I'm certain that you are all very hungry. So I've arranged a special lunch of cheese and bread for all of you."

How everyone enjoyed lunch that day! Afterwards, we put on our cloaks and bonnets and went out into the garden.

Water from an icy rain had soaked the ground, and the winter air was cold. The grass and the garden had frozen over. Most of the girls huddled together close to the building to try to keep warm. Many had coughs that continued all day and into the night.

One of the girls with a bad cough was the one with the red curls who had been sitting beside me in the schoolroom. Now she was braving the cold, seated on a stone bench, reading. I had always been shy when meeting new people, but since I liked reading too, I asked, "What is your book called?"

That simple question was to open my heart to my first true friend. Her name was Helen Burns. Our conversation went from books to our lives. Helen was a few years older, but like me, her parents were dead. She had been placed at Lowood, she explained, a charity home for educating orphans.

She Was Braving the Cold.

"Who pays if we have no money?" I asked.

"Many generous people from all over England. But the lady who has been the most generous is Naomi Brocklehurst. Her son manages the money that is donated to support the school. He's the one who buys all our clothes and food, and decides what we eat."

"And what about the teachers, do you like them?"

"Most are nice enough except for Miss Scatherd who teaches history and grammar. She has a bad temper and sometimes she's mean. But then there's Miss Temple. When you're with her, you can forget mean Miss Scatherd."

Our dinner that evening was just as bad as breakfast. I ate what I could, which wasn't much. Prayers followed, then a half-hour of recreation before bed.

This was my first day at Lowood.

CHAPTER 3

Life at Lowood School

The next day began like the first one except that we couldn't wash because the water in the basins had frozen. When it was time for breakfast, the porridge wasn't burnt, but the portions were so small, I wished there was more.

Since everyone shared the same room for their lessons, I could hear Miss Scatherd's class reading English history while I practiced my sewing. My new friend Helen was the target of Miss Scatherd's anger, as she was every day.

"Burns, hold your head up!" or "Burns, lift your chin!"or "Burns, stand up straight!"

She Never Received One Word of Praise.

When she was called upon, Helen always had all the correct answers. Yet, she never received one word of praise from the nasty Miss Scatherd. In fact, after Helen answered a very hard question, Miss Scatherd suddenly lashed out at her. "You dirty, unpleasant girl! Why didn't you wash your hands this morning?"

When Helen didn't offer an explanation, I thought to myself, Why doesn't she tell the teacher that the water was frozen and none of us could wash?

As my anger grew, I wondered why Helen didn't say a word or shed a tear. She just stood there, unmoving.

I didn't get a chance to talk to Helen until we had our play hour in the evening. "Why is Miss Scatherd so cruel to you?" I asked.

But Helen defended her. "She isn't cruel. She just wants to correct my faults and give me an education."

"Well, if I were in your place, I'd shout back."

"No, you wouldn't, Jane. Mr. Brocklehurst

would expel you from school, and then where would you go? Besides, the Bible teaches us to answer evil with good. Those are just Miss Scatherd's ways of teaching us, just as Miss Temple teaches us with kindness and praise."

I shook my head.

"You will change your mind when you're older, Jane. The Bible tells us to love our enemies."

"I cannot. If someone hates me then I must hate them, just as I hate Aunt Reed and her son John." Then I told Helen about my life suffering at Gateshead.

My first four months at Lowood were the cold winter months. We were made to spend time outdoors, but our clothes were too thin to protect us from the cold. We had no gloves or boots, and our hands and feet became raw and swollen. We never had enough food.

We walked two miles every Sunday in the bitter cold and snow to the church where Mr. Brocklehurst preached. He had not visited Lowood during my first month there, but the day he did became a day of horror for me.

"Those Are Just Miss Scatherd's Ways."

Mr. Brocklehurst entered our schoolroom. I remembered the warnings Aunt Reed had given him—the lies she had told about me. I remembered his promise to warn all my teachers about me. So when I saw him whispering to Miss Temple, I panicked. But I was close enough to hear him. He was scolding Miss Temple.

"I see from the bills that you gave the girls bread and cheese for lunch one day last month. Who gave you permission to spend that money?"

"I did that on my own, sir," explained Miss Temple. "Their breakfast porridge had been burnt and no one could eat it. I couldn't let the girls starve until dinner."

"Madam," he said, raising his voice, "these girls are not to be raised in luxury. They must learn to deprive themselves, to do without, to suffer, even to starve in order to become good people."

Miss Temple did not reply. Instead, she watched Mr. Brocklehurst's eyes as they traveled around the room. When they reached

Helen Burns, he demanded, "Miss Temple, why is this girl allowed to have such curls?"

"Helen's hair curls naturally."

"Girls must keep their hair short and straight. It must be cut off at once! And so must all the other girls who are so vain that they must have curls or twist their hair into braids."

While Mr. Brocklehurst was criticizing Miss Temple and the girls, I tried to hide by holding my writing slate in front of my face and doing my arithmetic. Somehow, the slate slipped out of my hands and crashed to the floor. Every head turned to me as I bent to pick up the pieces.

"Who is this careless girl?" demanded Mr. Brocklehurst as he pointed his cane at me. "Aha! It is the new pupil. Come up here onto this stool."

I froze with fear, but two older girls dragged me off my chair and lifted me onto a high stool in front of Mr. Brocklehurst. It brought me up as high as he was tall. With his cane still pointing at me, he spoke to the entire

"Do Not Talk to Her!"

room. "This girl may look innocent, but she has the devil in her. I must warn you to keep away from her. Do not play with her, do not talk to her, do not believe the lies she tells!"

"How shocking!" Miss Scatherd gasped to the other teachers.

"And," continued Mr. Brocklehurst, "I learned of her evil deeds from the kind lady who took her in as an orphan and raised her as her own daughter, with her own pure children. Yet this girl repaid that dear, generous lady with wicked behavior. And she will do the same here if you give her a chance."

As he turned to leave, Mr. Brocklehurst ordered, "Let her stand on that stool for another hour. No one is to speak to her for the rest of the day."

I didn't know how I could bear the shame I felt, not from Mr. Brocklehurst's words, but from having to stand on that stool for everyone to look at me. I began to shake. I felt my knees weaken. I had really been trying to be so good at Lowood, to make friends and do well in my

studies. And I had succeeded in doing both
But now I was beaten down again.

I lost count of how long I had been standing
there with my head down, sobbing, when I suddenly saw two feet standing in front of my stool. I
looked up and saw Helen Burns looking up at me.

"Your hour of punishment is ended," she
said, helping me down from the stool. She
handed me my breakfast of bread and coffee.

"Why are you so kind to me when everyone must hate me?" I asked her.

"No one hates you," she said gently. "I'm
certain they all probably pity you."

"Pity me? After what Mr. Brocklehurst
said?"

"His words are not God's words," Helen
said firmly. "And Mr. Brocklehurst himself is
not liked here, either by the girls or by the
teachers. I'm certain they don't believe anything he says."

Just then, a door opened at the end of the
schoolroom and Miss Temple entered. "I came
to find you, Jane," she said. "Please come with

"Your Punishment Is Ended."

me to my room. Helen, you may come too."

When we were seated in the cozy room in front of the fire, Miss Temple asked, "Are you over your grief, Jane?"

"I'm afraid I'll never be over it. I have been wrongly accused. Now you and everyone else will think I'm a wicked girl."

"We shall think what you have shown yourself to be and what you prove yourself to be," Miss Temple said gently. "Now, Jane, tell me about the lady Mr. Brocklehurst spoke about, the kind lady who raised you."

"She was my uncle's wife. I was too young to remember my uncle very well, but when he died he left me in her care. I often heard the servants say that she didn't want to raise me, but he had made her promise as he lay dying."

"Jane, I want to hear from you exactly what you do remember," Miss Temple said firmly. "Don't tell me any lies or exaggerate anything that happened."

So I began the story of my sad life. I tried my best not to let my anger influence my telling. When

I got to the point in my story where I mentioned Mr. Lloyd, the pharmacist, Miss Temple interrupted.

"I know Mr. Lloyd and I shall write to him. If he confirms what you have told me of the red room, I will see to it that everyone here believes you. But for now, Jane, I want you to know that I believe you completely."

I was overjoyed at Miss Temple's kindness. We sat for a while by the fire talking, and Miss Temple served us tea and cakes. Never in my life had I spent such a warm, happy evening with people who truly cared about me. I listened eagerly as Helen and Miss Temple spoke of books and people and places. The only worry I had was when Helen began to cough. She clutched at her chest for several long minutes until the hard coughing passed.

It was a week later that Miss Temple assembled the entire school and announced, "I've checked out the charges made against Jane Eyre and I'm happy to tell you she has been completely cleared. Everything you were told about her was a lie!"

53

My teachers shook hands with me and the girls crowded around me to congratulate me.

From that day on, with this new encourage-ment and new friends, I began to succeed at my lessons. Because of my excellent grades, I was given the opportunity, usually reserved for the older students, to start learning French, to play the piano, and to develop my skills at drawing.

I also learned a very important lesson that was to stay with me for life: It was better to eat small portions of poor food where I was sur-rounded by love, than to feast on fine food where I was surrounded by hatred.

So with all the hardships I endured at Lowood, I had made friends who cared about me. That was certainly much better than eat-ing the food served at Gateshead, where misery and hatred were all I had ever known.

CHAPTER 4

Death Comes to Lowood

Spring came, and life at Lowood improved. Flowers and trees bloomed everywhere.

But sadly, spring also brought an outbreak of typhus to Lowood. It was a disease that struck with high fever, rashes, terrible headaches and even delirium. The illness turned Lowood School into a hospital.

The neglected winter colds, unclean conditions and near starvation led to the typhus. It took its toll on forty-five out of the eighty girls there. Those who had friends or relatives were sent to them; those of us who were still well stayed at Lowood. The teachers were busy caring for the sick. Miss Temple spent her days and nights in the sickroom. She slept only two or three hours each day, sitting in a chair beside her patients.

One of the sick girls was my dear friend Helen, but she was not in the big sickroom with the other girls. I learned that she was in another room by herself with a disease called tuberculosis. Since I was only ten at the time, I had no idea how serious that illness was, or how it could destroy a person's lungs and bones. I simply thought it was a mild illness and that in time Helen would recover.

I began to realize how seriously ill Helen was when I saw Miss Temple carry her into the garden on a warm May day. Helen was wrapped in a blanket. As I started to run towards her, Miss Temple stopped me. "You must not come near her."

I froze on the path as I suddenly realized that Helen must be very ill indeed. "No, no! It can't be!" I sobbed. My shock turned to grief.

Helen Was Wrapped in a Blanket.

"I must find a way to see her!"

That night, I learned that Helen was being cared for in Miss Temple's room. I hurried across the dark halls. The door was open slightly. I poked my head in to make sure Miss Temple wasn't there. Then I saw Helen lying, unmoving, in a small bed beside Miss Temple's empty one.

"Helen, are you awake?" I whispered, moving closer.

Helen stirred and turned to me. A sad smile crossed her pale, thin face. "Is that you, Jane?"

I climbed onto her small bed and touched her forehead. It was cold; so were her cheeks and hands. But her warm smile was there for me, just as it had always been.

"Why are you here, Jane?" she asked weakly. "It is so late. I heard the clock strike eleven."

"I came to see you, Helen. I couldn't sleep until I had spoken to you."

"Dear Jane, do not be sad. My illness isn't painful, just"—her words were interrupted by a fit of coughing.

It was daylight when I found Miss Temple.

I Hurried Across the Dark Halls.

"Is she…is Helen dead?" I whispered.

"Yes, child, she is with God."

It was the worst moment of my life. Everything that had happened to me before, all the misery and humiliation at Gateshead, were as nothing to me now. I had suffered, but at the hands of people who cared nothing for me, and I nothing for them. Now I had lost the first, and the dearest friend I had ever had.

With Helen, I had shared all of my hopes and dreams. We had talked about so many things, and she had thus opened the world for me. From Helen I had learned that this world was a bigger, and better, place than Gateshead or Lowood, that there was beauty and splendor beyond what I had known.

I could never be as good a person as she was. The humiliations that we had both faced at the hands of Mr. Brocklehurst had shown me that. Helen could suffer anything and take it as God's will, and accept it. I never could. But in every other way, I would cling to everything she had taught me, and remember her forever.

I couldn't believe Helen was gone.

I had lost the only true friend I had ever had. All my other sorrows felt like nothing compared with this loss.

Helen was buried in a nearby churchyard, covered by a small mound of grass. It wasn't until fifteen years later that I was able to come back and place a marble headstone with her name on her grave.

CHAPTER 5

Leaving Lowood Behind

I stayed at Lowood for the next eight years. The typhus outbreak and the number of deaths it caused resulted in public outrage. An investigation revealed that Mr. Brocklehurst was responsible for the poor food, the polluted water, and the inadequate clothing. It was discovered that he had taken the money people had been donating to the school and using it for his own luxurious lifestyle.

Once a new manager for the school was put in charge, conditions improved. I got a good education during the next six years I spent at Lowood as a pupil. After that, I became a teacher there for two years. During those eight years, Miss Temple became my governess, my mother and my companion all in one.

When I turned eighteen, Miss Temple left Lowood to get married. After she had moved away, I no longer desired to stay at the school. The real world was out there and I wondered if I had the courage to go out and explore it.

I was tired of my lonely life at Lowood. I wanted a new and exciting one that I could enjoy. But to get this life, I would need a job to support myself. How do I go about getting a job? I asked myself.

Then, as if a wise fairy entered my brain and spoke to me, I cried out, "Yes! I will advertise in the newspaper for a position."

The advertisement I wrote said: *A young lady with two years of teaching experience is seeking a position with a family whose children are under fourteen.* (Since I was only eighteen myself, I didn't think it was a good idea to teach older children.) *Skilled in teaching English, French, drawing, sewing and music.*

Miss Temple Left Lowood.

About a week after my ad appeared, I received one reply. It was from a Mrs. Fairfax at an estate called Thornfield Hall. She asked for references, explained that the child in the home was a little girl of ten, and that the position paid thirty pounds a year. That was twice what I had been earning as a teacher at Lowood.

Since I had performed my duties very well at Lowood, the supervisors there gave me excellent references. Within two weeks I had packed my trunk, the same one I had brought with me eight years ago from Gateshead.

On the day before I left, I received a letter from Bessie, the only person who had shown me any kindness at Gateshead. She had learned where I was only because Aunt Reed had received a letter of reference about me.

Bessie wrote: *I am married and have two children, but I still work for the Reed family. I am happy, but sadly the family is not.*

Eliza and Georgiana still live at home with their mother and fight every day. John went off to college, but was expelled for bad behavior.

A Letter from Bessie

He is just throwing away his life and his mother's money as well.

She went on to explain something she knew would be of interest to me: *Mrs. Reed had a visit some years ago from a Mr. Eyre, who said he was your uncle. He was a wine merchant. He wanted to see you before sailing thousands of miles away on a ship to Madeira, a wine-producing island off the coast of Portugal, where he planned to live.*

Mrs. Reed always said your father's family was poor and to be despised, but Mr. Eyre seemed quite wealthy. He was much more of a gentleman than John Reed or any of their family's friends.

I packed Bessie's letter in my trunk, planning to answer it when I got to my new job. It was a link to an old friend and to family I never knew I had.

CHAPTER 6

A New Life Begins at Thornfield

It was very late at night when the coach slowed down, then stopped in front of high gates set into a tall stone wall. Behind the wall, at the end of a long drive, stood a huge three-story manor house.

"This is Thornfield Hall, ma'am," said the driver.

Inside, waiting to greet me was a smiling, gray-haired woman. "You must be Jane Eyre, the new governess," she said, reaching her arms out to me. "I'm Mrs. Fairfax. You must be cold and tired, my dear. Come, let us go into

"You Must Be Jane Eyre."

the drawing room. You can warm yourself by the fire and I'll order some food for you."

While I ate, Mrs. Fairfax explained that my future pupil was named Adele Varens. She was a ten-year-old girl who had come to live at Thornfield only a few months earlier.

"Then she is related to you?" I asked.

"Oh, no, dear. Sadly, I have no family. I manage the household here for the master, Mr. Rochester. Adele's mother was a famous French actress and a close friend of the master's. When she died suddenly, Mr. Rochester brought Adele to live here, since she had no family to care for her. The master is a very kind, caring gentleman."

"I shall look forward to meeting Adele and Mr. Rochester tomorrow," I said.

"Oh, the master isn't here now. Mr. Rochester travels all over the world."

"Then I shall look forward to meeting Mr. Rochester when he returns," I said. I bid Mrs. Fairfax goodnight, and proceeded up the elegant oak staircase to my room.

My room looked charming by candlelight, but even more so the next morning in daylight when I saw pretty lace curtains, papered walls, a carpeted floor, delicately carved furniture and a comfortable armchair.

I was dressed in the simple black teaching clothes I had worn at Lowood when Mrs. Fairfax knocked at my door. She greeted me with a hug. "Come," she said, taking my arm. "I want you to meet Adele. She speaks French, which I know you do too, but Adele does quite well in English too."

We went into the nursery and were greeted by a little girl with a head full of dark curls. How those curls reminded me of my dear friend Helen!

Afterwards, one of the servants took Adele to the nursery to play. Mrs. Fairfax took me on a tour of the three floors of Thornfield Hall. "The third floor is not used much," she explained, as we headed back down.

It was then that I heard a strange, frightening laugh echoing through the halls above us.

The Day Was Sunny but Cold.

"What was that?" I asked in surprise.

"It must be one of the servants upstairs," Mrs. Fairfax said, a bit nervously. "Probably Grace Poole. She sometimes does her sewing chores in one of the rooms on the third floor. Once in a while Grace has been known to take a bit of a drink here and there. You need not be concerned."

I couldn't get that strange, frightening laugh out of my mind. I heard it often in the days and weeks that followed, along with other weird noises from the third floor.

And so the months passed. One January afternoon Adele seemed to be coming down with a cold. I let her stay in her room and play quietly. I took advantage of some free time and offered to take a letter into the village post office at Millcote for Mrs. Fairfax. The day was sunny but cold, and I walked the few miles quickly to keep warm.

It was on the way back in the late winter afternoon that I had an experience that would change my life forever.

From behind me on the deserted road, I heard the galloping of hooves. I moved to the side of the road to let the horse and rider gallop by. Running alongside them was a huge long-haired black-and-white dog. As the group passed me, the horse slipped on a small sheet of ice on the road, throwing its rider to the ground. The dog ran to its master. When the dog spotted me at the side of the road, it ran up to me as if to ask for help.

I hurried to the fallen man and knelt down. "Are you hurt, sir?" I asked.

The man mumbled some swear words to himself, but ignored me.

So I asked again. "Can I do anything to help you, sir?"

"You can move away," he snapped as he slowly got to his knees, then unsteadily to his feet. "Down, Pilot," he called to his barking dog.

I wanted to be helpful, so I tried again. "If you are hurt, sir, I can get someone from Thornfield or from the village to help you."

"Are You Hurt, Sir?"

"That's not necessary. Nothing is broken. It is only a sprain," he said gruffly as he waved me away.

"But I cannot leave you like this, sir, until I see if you can get back on your horse."

"You should be home yourself, young lady," he warned. "Night is coming fast. Do you live near here?"

"Yes, sir, at that large house with the towers," I replied, pointing to Thornfield in the distance.

"Whose house is that?" he asked.

"It belongs to a gentleman named Edward Rochester."

"And do you know Mr. Rochester?"

"No, sir. He is not there now."

"And are you a servant there?"

"No, sir. I am the governess."

"I see," he said. He tried to take a step toward his horse. His face twisted in pain and he groaned. "I suppose I'll need you to help me get on my horse."

So, leaning on my shoulder instead of on his sprained ankle, he managed to climb back into the saddle.

When I finally reached Thornfield about an hour later, I saw a huge, long-haired black-and-white dog sitting on a rug outside the library. "Pilot?" I whispered, almost to myself. Pilot came up to me, wagging his tail.

"Whose dog is this?" I asked Mrs. Fairfax, who was just coming out of the library.

"It is the master's. Mr. Rochester arrived home a short while ago. Unfortunately he had an accident, but he wasn't badly hurt. He sprained his ankle when his horse slipped on the ice and threw him off."

So that strange gentleman on the road was my master, Edward Rochester!

Mrs. Fairfax came into Adele's room and announced that Mr. Rochester wanted Adele and me to have tea with him in the dining room. Adele could not be held back.

As we entered the dining room, Adele ran to his chair. "This is Miss Eyre, sir," Mrs. Fairfax quietly announced.

"Let her be seated," he said, not even bothering to look up. He was concentrating on Adele on his lap and on Pilot at his feet. I felt

"Bring Miss Eyre Here."

rather uncomfortable at being ignored so completely. I quietly took a seat against the wall, away from where he was sitting.

"Bring Miss Eyre here," he said to Adele, "then go to my travel bag and find the presents I have for you."

Adele ran off. Mr. Rochester turned to me. "Sit here by the fire, Miss Eyre. Mrs. Fairfax tells me you came from Lowood School. I don't know how you managed to stay at such a place for eight years. Don't you have any family?"

"No, sir. My parents are dead and I have no sisters or brothers or aunts or uncles that I know of."

"And what did you think of Mr. Brocklehurst while he managed the school? Did you respect him?"

"Oh, no!" I cried. "I disliked him. So did all the girls. He starved us, made us wear rags, and forced the girls to cut off their hair. But worst of all, he frightened us with such terrible stories of death and hell that we were afraid to go to sleep at night."

"But surely you got an education, which you made use of when you stayed there to teach. Mrs. Fairfax showed me some of your watercolor landscapes and seascapes. What did you copy them from?"

"Copy them? Oh, no, sir. I create my paintings out of my head, sir, from my own imagination."

He suddenly got up and snapped at me. "Why are you letting Adele stay up so late? Take her to bed now!"

I thought to myself, What a strange man Mr. Rochester is. His moods change so quickly! It happened on the road, and now here again.

When I mentioned this to Mrs. Fairfax, she explained, "The master has had a great deal of pain in his life and many family troubles."

"But I thought he had no family," I said.

"Not now, but he did once. He had an older brother, Rowland, who plotted with their father against Mr. Edward. Both of them are dead now and Thornfield is Mr. Edward's. But

"What Did You Copy Them From?"

it holds many unhappy memories for him, so he stays away as much as possible."

When I asked Mrs. Fairfax more about the Rochester family, she claimed not to know anything else. I doubted it, but I didn't want to press her on the subject.

CHAPTER 7

Edward Rochester

Over the next few days, Mr. Rochester was busy with business callers or was out riding. When I did see him in the house, sometimes he would just nod coldly and other times he would smile. Again I thought, How strange!

When he finally sent word that Adele and I were to join him in the library one evening, we found him in his chair beside the fire. Adele ran to him while I waited just inside the door.

"Come forward and sit here," he said, smiling at me and pointing to the chair opposite him.

I obeyed and sat looking at him as he gazed into the fire.

Sometimes Friendly, Sometimes Cold

Suddenly he turned and asked sharply, "Why are you examining me, Miss Eyre? Do you find me ugly...or perhaps handsome?"

I wondered if he had had too much wine at dinner for to ask such a personal question about the feelings of an employee. But before I could decide on a proper answer, he spoke again.

"I sent for you to find out more about you. I am a difficult man to work for. You may be uncomfortable working for me at times when I'm not as friendly and talkative as I am tonight."

I remained silent but my gaze never left his face.

"Come, come, Miss Eyre, I sent for you for conversation. I did not send for Adele, who is perfectly content to sit still watching the fire. It is conversation with you that I wish, so speak."

"What about, sir?" I asked with a smile.

"Whatever you like. I leave the words and thoughts up to you."

I remained silent, but continued to smile.

"Are you deaf, Miss Eyre? Or just stubborn?" Then he bent toward me and looked right into my eyes.

"I have been behaving badly, haven't I?" he said, returning my smile. "I know that even though I'm thirty-eight, old enough to be your father, I have no right to order you to speak. Nor do I have that right just because you work for me. So now I ask you—not order you— would you be kind enough to talk to me, Miss Eyre?"

"Sir, I would be happy to have a conversation with you. Simply ask me your questions."

He sat back in his chair, but the smile never left his face. "Do you ever let your smile become a laugh, Miss Eyre? No, don't answer. I don't think you are naturally so serious. I hope, in time, you will be comfortable enough here so that you can be your natural self."

"But, sir," I began.

"No, Miss Eyre, let me go on. You seem to me like a bird in a cage, restless to be free so you can soar high above the clouds." With that, he turned his back to me and spoke into the fire. "You may leave now, Miss Eyre, and take Adele with you. We shall talk further at another time."

My next meeting with Mr. Rochester came some days later. I was taking Adele for a walk in the garden. As we turned a corner, I caught sight of him leaning against a tree, staring back at Thornfield. Actually, his head was tilted back so his gaze was concentrated on the third floor. As we got closer, I saw that his stare was more of a glare, with his face twisted in pain and disgust.

"I hate it," he said quietly to me as he saw us approach. But before I could say a word, he turned away from us and went back into the house.

I thought to myself, There is something in my master's past that makes him hate his family home. He is moody and often angry over it. It is so sad. How I wish I could ease his grief.

These feelings stayed with me long after I had put Adele to bed. Once I was in my own room, seated in my comfortable arm-chair, thoughts of Mr. Rochester whirled around in my brain. What causes him to hate

"Who's There?" I Cried.

this house so much? What makes him leave it so often and stay away for such long periods of time? The past eight weeks have been the longest he has ever stayed home.

Somehow, the idea of Mr. Rochester leaving again made me catch my breath. I suddenly realized, If he leaves, my days will be without joy. I will miss him terribly!

I must have fallen asleep in my chair with dreams of Edward Rochester filling my brain. I was suddenly wakened by eerie moans from outside my room. I heard the clock in the downstairs hall strike two. Then the handle on my door began to rattle.

"Who's there?" I cried, jumping up, chilled with fear.

My answer was a demonic laugh coming through the keyhole of my door. The laugh was followed by gurgles and moans and then, complete silence.

Next, I heard footsteps walking away from my door and climbing the staircase that led

"What's Going On?" He Gasped.

to the third floor.

With trembling hands, I opened my door. A candle was sitting on the floor in the hallway outside my door. How strange, I thought. No one usually leaves a lighted candle in the hall overnight.

Then I smelled something burning. It was not the candle. I looked around quickly and saw smoke coming from Mr. Rochester's room. I ran to his door and flung it open. The curtains around his bed were covered in flames. In the middle of the bed lay my master in a deep sleep.

"Wake up! Wake up!" I cried as I ran to the bed and began to shake him. Then I realized that the smoke had left him unconscious. Not a moment could be lost! The sheets were beginning to catch fire as well.

I rushed to his water pitcher and wash-basin, which were both filled. I heaved them up and emptied them onto the bed and the sleeping man. It was enough to put out the flames on the bed and enough to finally waken Mr. Rochester.

"What's going on?" he gasped, in between

spitting out water and coughing up smoke.

"There has been a fire, sir," I explained, still trembling from the horror of the experience. "But I've put it out. Someone deliberately set this fire. You must find out who it is."

Then I told him about the strange laughter and moans I had heard in the hallway, the footsteps going up to the third floor, and how I smelled the smoke coming from his room.

"Sit down here, Jane," he said as he seated me in an armchair. He put on his robe, then wrapped my trembling body in his heavy cloak. "I must go up to the third floor and investigate. Do not leave this room or call anyone."

I waited a long while, getting colder and colder. Finally, he returned.

"You say you have heard this odd laugh before, Jane?" he asked.

"Yes, sir. Mrs. Fairfax says it's a servant named Grace Poole who does her sewing up on the third floor."

"Yes, she is a strange one. But since I'm not hurt, no one in the house needs to know

Grace Poole Was Strange.

what happened. I'll simply explain that I fell asleep with my candle burning."

Mr. Rochester blocked my way and took my hand. "You saved my life tonight, Jane," he whispered through lips that trembled as he spoke.

I gently pulled my hand away as I, too, began to tremble. "I'm glad I was awake, sir."

I hurried from the room, eager to be back in my own bed. But I was not to sleep. I could not sleep that night, for my thoughts were overflowing with Edward Rochester's touch on my hand and the trembling of his lips as he thanked me.

I learned the following morning that my master had slept on the library sofa that night. On my way to breakfast, I saw the servants cleaning his room. Even Grace Poole was there, sitting in his armchair sewing new bed curtains. She looked up as I stopped in the doorway and quite calmly said, "Good morning, ma'am."

How can she be so calm? I wondered. After all, she was obviously the one whose laughter I heard and who probably started the fire.

94

I must put her to a test, I decided. So I asked her, "Did anything happen here last night? I thought I heard some noise."

"The master was reading in bed last night and fell asleep with his candle lit," she answered calmly. "It set fire to his bed curtains, but luckily he woke and put out the flames."

"And no one heard it?" I probed deeper.

But Grace had a reasonable explanation. "All the servants sleep on the other side of the house. Did you hear anything?"

"I heard some strange laughter."

"You must have been dreaming, Miss Eyre," she said with a sympathetic smile.

How innocent she sounded and how calmly she spoke. I ended the conversation at that point and took Adele down to breakfast. Still, I couldn't stop wondering why Mr. Rochester hadn't accused Grace or even fired her. And why did he make me promise not to tell anyone?

In a jealous moment, which I had never experienced in my life before, I even wondered

My Heart Cannot Believe That.

if there was a romance between Grace Poole and Mr. Rochester. But no, I decided. My heart cannot believe that, not after the way he looked at me and held my hand, I thought.

Adele noticed that my hand began to tremble as I helped her with her drawing lesson. I found myself listening for my master's voice or his footsteps. But I didn't hear either.

It wasn't until I was having tea with Mrs. Fairfax that evening that I learned that Mr. Rochester had left Thornfield shortly after breakfast.

"Will he be back tonight?" I asked.

"That isn't likely. He's gone to a big party a distance away at Eshton Hall. He may very well be gone a week or two. A gentleman like Mr. Rochester is in great demand as a house-guest. All the ladies are very fond of him, and some, I hear, are interested in him romantically."

"And will these ladies be at Eshton Hall?"

"Certainly. Mr. and Mrs. Eshton have three daughters, all elegant young ladies. Also there is Blanche Ingram, who is one of the most beautiful women I have ever seen."

At that moment, Mrs. Fairfax was called away. I had time to search my heart and my feelings.

"What a fool you are, Jane Eyre!" I scolded myself. "How could you think that such a man could have romantic feelings about you? He could never marry someone like you, an orphan with no family or fortune, a plain-looking, simple governess!"

To stop my crazy thoughts that Edward Rochester could ever love me, I went to my room and took out my drawing pad. I sat in front of a mirror. On the left half of the paper, I sketched my reflection: plain, unattractive Jane Eyre. Then on the right half, I sketched what I imagined Blanche Ingram to look like, using Mrs. Fairfax's description of the young lady's beauty.

That way, if I ever started thinking romantic thoughts about Edward Rochester again, all I'd need to do would be to take out my drawing pad and stare at it. That would take me out of my dream world and back to the real one.

From Mrs. Fairfax's Description

CHAPTER 8

A Party at Thornfield

A week passed, then ten days. Even though I tried hard not to care, I found myself missing my master terribly.

It didn't help at all when Mrs. Fairfax commented, "I wouldn't be surprised if the master went from Eshton Hall to London and even to Europe, and not come back for a year."

When I heard that, my heart sank, but I quickly let my head take control and I reminded myself: Jane, you must remember that the master only pays your salary for teaching Adele. He has no other ties to you. He does not want your love, so don't deceive yourself.

100

I went about my duties with Adele for the next few days, wondering if it might be better for me to leave Thornfield and find a governess position elsewhere.

Then, fifteen days after Mr. Rochester's departure, Mrs. Fairfax received a letter from him. It was brought in while we were at breakfast. She opened it and began to read.

"Mr. Rochester will be returning in three days, on Thursday," she announced, then added, "and not alone. All the guests from Eshton Hall are coming too. I'm to prepare all the rooms and hire more kitchen and cleaning help. We shall have a full house."

Over the next three days, Thornfield was aired and scrubbed, painted and polished. Adele was allowed a break from her lessons since I was needed to help Mrs. Fairfax with the baking and cooking. It was during this busy time that I happened to walk into the kitchen just after Grace Poole had left to go upstairs. Two of the servants were talking about her.

The Sound of Horses Reached Me.

"Mealtime's the only time she leaves that room," said one. "Otherwise, she's up there the whole day and night."

"But she must be very well paid for it," said the other. "Besides, nobody else would do that job." The woman turned and saw me entering the kitchen. She hurriedly continued in a whisper, "Does she know?"

The woman shook her head "no."

So I was right after all! I thought. There is a mystery here and for some reason, I'm not supposed to know about it.

I didn't have time to dwell on this mystery for it was already Thursday. Mrs. Fairfax put on her best satin gown and had me dress Adele in her prettiest party dress. I didn't change from my plain daytime governess dress, for I did not expect to leave the schoolroom.

At six o'clock that evening, the sound of horses and carriages reached me. I hurried to the window. I stood to the side so I wouldn't be seen by anyone below.

Mr. Rochester was riding his black horse and beside him on an equally handsome white horse rode a beautiful lady. Her long purple riding dress almost swept the ground, and the veil on her hat streamed in the breeze, revealing long, satiny black curls that framed her face.

Minutes later, several carriages pulled up, announcing the arrival of the other guests.

Adele was in her party dress. She was upset that the guests were getting ready to go down to dinner and she wasn't allowed to join them.

"It's only for grown-ups, dear," I explained gently. "I will go and bring up some dinner for both of us. Perhaps later Mr. Rochester will send for you."

I left, carefully taking the back stairs directly to the kitchen. There was great bustle there with dinner preparations. I quickly made up two plates of food for Adele and myself, and hurried back.

I let Adele stay up past her bedtime and although the master hadn't sent for her, I eased

The Guests Were Getting Ready for Dinner.

her disappointment by letting her sit at the top of the stairs.

The next day, I saw Blanche Ingram and Mr. Rochester laughing together on horseback as they rode out, side by side.

I commented about this when I saw Mrs. Fairfax later. "Mr. Rochester evidently prefers Miss Ingram to any of the other ladies here. But I haven't had the opportunity yet to see her up close."

"You will this evening, Jane," she told me. "I explained to Mr. Rochester how much Adele wanted to spend a little time with the ladies. He said he'll let her come into the drawing room after dinner. And he said, 'Tell Miss Eyre that I wish her to accompany Adele.'"

"He was just being polite," I replied. "I don't really have to go."

"Yes you do, my dear. Mr. Rochester said those exact words. And he also said, 'If she refuses, tell her I shall come upstairs and carry her down myself.'"

"He needn't do that," I said laughing. "I'll go, but will you be there with me?"

"No, Jane. I begged off and he said it was all right. I suggest you go into the drawing room while everyone is still at dinner and find yourself a seat in a quiet corner. You only have to stay until Mr. Rochester sees you. Then you can slip away."

Why was Mr. Rochester so insistent on my being in the drawing room that night? The question bothered me the entire day.

That evening I did as Mrs. Fairfax suggested. I took a window seat partly hidden by the curtains. Adele seated herself on a stool at my feet, too excited to sit still, but trying her best not to wrinkle her party dress.

When the ladies entered, I rose and curtsied. One or two of them nodded to me, but the others, including Blanche Ingram and her mother, ignored me.

It is interesting to note, dear reader, that Lady Ingram reminded me a great deal of Aunt Reed, so I had two reasons to particularly dislike her.

She Just Talked to Get Attention.

Blanche Ingram matched the description Mrs. Fairfax had given me, but she resembled even more the drawing I had made of her, even though I had never seen her. The only thing missing from my sketch was the arrogance in her face when she spoke to people, except when she spoke to the master.

Miss Ingram was eager to show off not only her fine singing voice and her ability to speak French, but also how much smarter she was than the other ladies. However, the topics she chose to talk about showed me that she wasn't really smart at all. She just talked to get attention.

When the gentlemen entered the drawing room after the ladies were seated, I tried my best to keep my eyes on my needlework. But I failed. As I looked up to gaze on Mr. Rochester's strikingly powerful face, I could not forget his strong hand holding mine and his eyes full of love as he looked down at me.

Please understand, reader, I did not intend to fall in love with Edward Rochester. Surely you know how hard I tried not to. But I knew then that while there was breath left in my body, I would always love him.

The gentlemen took seats in the drawing room, while my master stood by the hearth, leaning his arm on the mantel.

Blanche Ingram immediately came over to join him and circled his free arm with hers. "Edward," she said loud enough for all to hear, "I thought you weren't fond of children."

"I'm not," he replied, frowning.

"Then why did you take over the care of that little girl?" She pointed her jeweled fingers at Adele.

"Her father ran away years ago and she was left alone when her mother died. Adele's mother was a dear friend of mine. The child had no one else to take her in."

"You should have sent her to an orphan's school, not hired a governess and have to support both of them."

I hoped that Miss Ingram's mention of me would turn Edward's eyes in my direction, but he simply told her, "I never thought of it."

I Would Always Love Him.

However, Blanche Ingram was not finished with the subject. "Well, let me tell you, Edward, I had at least a dozen governesses when I was growing up, half of them hateful and the other half stupid. And judging by that one's looks"—and she pointed to me—"I see all the faults of a woman who works in that position."

One of the ladies, who was tired of Miss Ingram's cruelty, interrupted by asking the master, "Dear Edward, are you in good voice tonight to sing for us?"

"Yes, Edward, do," pleaded Lady Ingram. "And I shall play for you."

Now is my time to slip away, I told myself. But the moment Mr. Rochester started to sing, I sat frozen until he finished. Everyone applauded and crowded around him with praise and compliments.

I told Adele to stay on her stool until the master sent her upstairs. Then I quietly made my way to the door and into the hall. I was hurrying to the staircase when I heard the drawing room door open and close behind me. The next instant I was standing face to face with Mr. Rochester.

"Why didn't you come and speak to me inside, Jane?"

"You were so busy, sir. I didn't wish to disturb you."

"Disturb? You are the one who seems disturbed, Jane. You are much paler than when I left. Did you catch a cold from getting wet when you put out the fire in my room?"

"Not at all, sir."

"Then come back to the drawing room."

"I am tired, sir."

"No, Jane. You are upset, so much so that your eyes are filling with tears. But this is not the time to discuss it, with servants going in and out of the rooms. I expect you to come down with my guests every evening. And for now, good night my dar—"

He stopped, then turned and left me standing there.

CHAPTER 9

The Gypsy Fortune-Teller

Over the next several evenings, I had to sit in the drawing room for hours and watch Mr. Rochester and Miss Ingram whisper to each other, exchange broad smiles, and even hold hands. I observed them as teammates when the guests put on costumes and makeup and played charades. Each team took turns trying to act out mystery words for the rest to guess.

Though I was forced to watch Mr. Rochester and Miss Ingram together constantly, I couldn't stop loving him. I couldn't "unlove" him. But as the days wore on, I became more and more certain that he would marry her. I realized that while Blanche Ingram was beautiful on the outside, inside she was vain and selfish. She showed no kindness to anyone and no tenderness or pity toward Adele.

I was certain that Mr. Rochester was aware of Miss Ingram's faults, so why would he want to marry her?

If she were a good and noble lady, I said to myself, I might admit that she was worthy of Mr. Rochester's love.

One morning I learned that my master had been called away to Millcote on business. His guests kept themselves busy that day, the women doing their needlepoint or playing cards and the men playing billiards or horseback riding.

After lunch, one of the men suggested a walk to see a gypsy camp near a nearby town. But when it started to rain, the outing was postponed.

By dusk, everyone was back in the drawing room when a coach was heard pulling up to the front door. Adele ran to the window and cried, "Oh, Mr. Rochester is home!"

Blanche Ingram hurried to the window

and pushed Adele aside. "You nasty child!" she cried. "Why did you lie to us? It is not Mr. Rochester getting out. It is someone else." And she glared at me.

Mrs. Fairfax led the stranger in and introduced him. "This is Mr. Richard Mason, who has just arrived to see Mr. Rochester."

Mr. Mason was a tall, well dressed gentleman about the same age as my master. But where Mr. Rochester had a strong face and commanding eyes, this man had dull eyes with a faraway look, and small, weak lips.

"It is unfortunate that I have traveled such a long distance to see Edward only to learn that he is not here," said Mr. Mason. "But since we have been friends for so long, it should be no problem for me to stay until he returns."

Mr. Mason soon made himself comfortable in conversation with the other gentlemen in the room. I heard him explain that he was from the island of Jamaica in the Caribbean. "Yes, that was where I first met Edward," he said.

Mrs. Fairfax Led the Stranger In.

"This Is Mr. Richard Mason."

In the middle of this conversation, Sam, the Thornfield footman, came in to speak to Mrs. Fairfax. "A gypsy woman is at the kitchen door," he said. "She wants to come in and tell fortunes."

"Send her away," Mrs. Fairfax ordered. "We'll not have any of that nonsense here."

A few minutes later, Sam returned and announced, "That creature refuses to move from the door."

Lady Ingram, Blanche's mother, jumped up from her chair and exclaimed, "I refuse to be part of this disgrace!"

"But you will be part of it!" screamed Blanche. "You can't tell me what to do. I insist on having my fortune told."

But Blanche wasn't finished yet. Turning to Sam, she ordered, "Let the gypsy in. It will be wonderful fun."

When Sam returned, he was shaking his head as he said, "The gypsy refuses to come in here to the drawing room with what she calls the vulgar herd. Those were her words, sirs, not mine. She insists that people go in to see her one by one."

"Well, I shall not go into the kitchen," snapped Blanche. "Take her into the library, Sam. Find her a place to sit where she can't steal or dirty anything."

Sam did as he was told, then returned to the drawing room. "Further, the gypsy will only tell the fortunes of young, single ladies. She will not speak to their mothers, or to any of the gentlemen either."

"Then I shall go first!" cried Blanche.

"Oh, my dear child!" cried Lady Ingram, wringing her hands. "I beg you, do not go in there!" But her words fell on a closed door.

Everyone waited in silence as the time dragged by. Finally, after about fifteen minutes, the door opened and out walked Miss Ingram.

Everyone looked at her with eager curiosity, but she returned their questioning glances with cold stares. She didn't seem upset, but she didn't appear happy either. Her lips were clenched tightly as she walked stiffly to her seat and picked up a book.

"Well, what happened in there, Blanche?" demanded her mother.

"That gypsy is a witch who does the devil's work. She read my palm and told me what all palm readers tell, nothing different. But she should be jailed for begging, and for extorting money by pretending to be what she is not."

I thought to myself, the gypsy hasn't told her anything she wanted to hear.

When the other young ladies took their turns in the library, we could hear giggles and little shrieks of laughter coming through the walls. Upon their return, they shared their astonishment with all of us.

"She told us our names and things about our homes and our belongings," said one.

"She knows all about us," another added. "Our thoughts, our friends—even what we wished for in our lives!"

"One Single Lady Left"

Blanche pretended to be reading her book, although she hadn't turned a single page since she first sat down.

While I was absorbed in the scene of this "vulgar herd," as the gypsy had called them, Sam came up to me and spoke in a low voice. "The gypsy says there is still one single young lady left. She will not leave until she tells that lady's fortune. I guess she means you, Miss Eyre."

"Certainly, Sam, I will go," I answered. I was secretly eager to satisfy my curiosity.

The old gypsy woman was seated in an armchair near the fire. She wore a bright red cloak. Her black hat was tied under her chin with a striped handkerchief. Both partly hid her face. She seemed to be muttering to herself as she read from a little book in her hands. She looked up when I came in, revealing a strange dark face, locks of matted gray hair down her wrinkled cheeks. "So, you want your fortune told," she said in a gravelly voice.

"I don't really believe in the powers you claim to have, but go ahead if you

"Love Is Very Near You."

wish. I shall listen."

"Aha!" cried the gypsy. "Your footsteps told me to expect you to be stubborn. Perhaps you will believe in my powers when I tell you that you are cold, you are sick and you are silly."

"How foolish of you!" I argued. "You have no way of proving your words."

"I say you are cold because you are alone with no one to warm your heart. I say you are sick because you don't let love come close to you. And I say you are silly because when you did find love, you did not take one step to welcome it and meet it. Yet love is very near you, within your reach. Do you have such a hope for your future?"

"The only hope I have is to save enough money from my salary to open up a school someday in a little house of my own."

"Is that all you think about when you sit on your window seat in the drawing room?" she asked slyly.

"How do you know where I sit?" I demanded, concealing my surprise.

"I told you I have great powers. And when you look at everyone in that room, is there one person who gets more of your attention than the others? Is it a gentleman who also gets the attention of a beautiful woman in that room?"

"I don't know any of the gentlemen in that room."

"You don't know the master of the house?"

As the gypsy kept getting closer and closer to the truth about my feelings, I felt my heart start to flutter.

But the gypsy didn't stop. "And haven't you even pictured him married to that beautiful woman?"

"No, no!" I cried, trying to deny even to myself how close the gypsy came to the truth of my feelings. "Your fortune-telling skills are not as good as you claim."

"Ah, but you know that Mr. Rochester is to be married to the beautiful Miss Ingram. He surely must love her, and she probably loves him or at least his money. I know she considers the Rochester estate quite desirable. But when

I hinted to her that it might not be what she expected, she turned very serious. I suspect that if some gentleman came along with a larger fortune than Mr. Rochester's, she would leave him in an instant."

"Enough, gypsy!" I interrupted. "I came to hear my fortune, not Mr. Rochester's."

"Your fortune is not clear. I see happiness for you, but you must reach out your hand, and your heart, and take it."

Suddenly, the gypsy raised her hand and forcefully pointed to the door. "Leave, Miss Eyre. My powers are weakening. Your fortune-telling session is over."

I stood up, but did not leave immediately. I stared at that raised hand. It wasn't the dried-up hand of an old gypsy woman, but a strong, broad hand, with a familiar ring glowing on the little finger.

"I know that ring!" I gasped. "I've seen it a hundred times before." My eyes followed that hand as it turned back to its owner to pull off the gypsy hat and cloak.

"The Devil You Say!"

It was Mr. Rochester!

"I'll go now," I said, rather annoyed at him. "I should just tell you that there's a gentleman here to see you. A Mr. Mason."

"Mason!" he shouted. "The devil you say!"

"Yes, sir," I replied.

He cursed under his breath. "Just bring Mason to me," he said at last. "Then leave us alone."

I Was Awakened in the Dead of Night.

CHAPTER 10

The Mysterious Mr. Mason

I delivered my master's message to Mr. Mason and I led him to the library. I went up to my room. But I was not to have a restful sleep.

I was awakened in the dead of night by a sharp, shrill cry that seemed to fill the entire house. My pulse stopped, my heart stood still. From the third floor room above my head, I heard a wild struggle and a man's voice crying, "Help! Help! Rochester, come help me!"

Next, I heard a door open and shut quickly, then footsteps running through the hall and up the steps to the third floor. Afterwards there was only silence.

In Case I Was Needed

I put on a robe and ran from my room. The other guests had gathered in the darkened hallway as well. They were all confused and terrified.

Moments later, a candle appeared on the staircase to the third floor. As the flame moved down the steps, it lit Mr. Rochester as he came down to the second floor where we were all gathered. "Nothing is wrong. One of the servants had a nightmare. Now go back to your rooms, before you catch a chill in this hallway."

They did as Mr. Rochester asked, but I knew his story was just to calm the guests. I went back to my room. Instead of going back to bed, I got dressed. I wanted to be ready in case I was needed for any emergencies.

It wasn't long after I had finished dressing that I heard a light tapping on my door. I knew it was him.

"Yes, come in."

"Gather some sponges and towels and smelling salts, and follow me. Do you get sick at the sight of blood?" he asked.

"No, sir," I said.

We entered a large, dark bedroom. Mr. Rochester pushed aside a huge tapestry on the wall, revealing a heavy iron door. He took a key from his pocket and inserted it in the lock.

"Wait here," he said as he stepped inside with the candle. He closed the door behind him.

From behind that door, I heard a snarling sound, almost like a menacing dog. It was followed by the hoarse voice of Grace Poole... then some whispers...then silence.

Minutes later, my master returned to the bedroom. He locked the iron door behind him. He pointed his candle to a large armchair. Mr. Mason's limp body was sprawled across it, with his head bent back and his eyes closed. His right shoulder and arm were soaked with blood.

As Mr. Mason opened his eyes, my master sponged away the blood from his arm and shoulder. "Am I going to die?" whispered Mr. Mason.

"No, foolish man. It's only a scratch. But I shall leave Miss Eyre with you while I go for the doctor. However, you must not speak one word to her," he warned. "If you do, I promise you that you will die…by my hand!"

Then he turned to me and said, "Sponge the blood away as I did and do not speak to him. This may puzzle you now, Jane, but just trust me and do as I say."

After Mr. Rochester left, I was alone with my fears, sitting by the armchair tending the wounded man and frightened of the wild beast behind the locked iron door.

Is that wild beast the same quiet servant I thought Grace Poole was? I asked myself. And what mysterious creature lives in Thornfield Hall, who starts a fire and now draws blood in the middle of the night? And what was Richard Mason doing up here when he had his own bedroom on the second floor? And why did my master order him not to speak to me, on penalty of death? And why did my master turn so pale when I told him last evening that Mr. Mason was here?

So many questions ran through my thoughts, but not one answer. All I could do

I Heard His Horse and Carriage.

was trust him, as my master had asked me to do. My patient's moans interrupted my thoughts. I looked toward the window to see the sun starting to rise. Mr. Rochester had been gone only two hours, but it seemed like a week. Finally, I heard his horse and carriage pull into the driveway.

When Mr. Rochester entered the room with Dr. Carter, my master ordered him to hurry and bandage the wound. "We must prepare him to leave in half an hour."

As the doctor was examining the wound, he told Mr. Mason, "You've got teeth marks on your shoulder and arms as well as knife wounds."

Mr. Mason explained weakly. "She looked so calm and quiet the moment before she bit me and stabbed me. I should have listened to Edward and not gone up alone. She probably would have killed me if he hadn't come running in and grabbed the knife from her. She actually threatened to drain the blood from my heart as well!"

The Carriage Pulled Up.

Mr. Rochester shuddered and tried to calm Mr. Mason. "Don't pay any attention to her wild gibberish, Richard. You will forget all about it as soon as you get back to Jamaica."

"It will be impossible to forget this night."

While Mr. Rochester and Dr. Carter helped Mr. Mason put on a clean shirt and his coat, I went downstairs to unlock the side door and have the carriage driver pull up to that entrance.

As he climbed into the coach, Mr. Mason leaned out and tearfully pleaded, "Take care of her, Edward, and treat her as gently as possible."

"I do my best as I have always done and always will," my master replied as he closed the coach door. He stepped back as it drove away.

I turned to go into the house, but my master stopped me. "Do not go back into that dungeon, Jane. Please, let us take a walk in the fresh air, where everything is sweet and pure."

As we walked in the garden, Mr. Rochester turned to me. "If only I could forget the past and start my life over again," he said, his voice filled with emotion.

"Trust in God to give you strength," I told him.

"No, Jane. It is you who gives me strength. Tell me, will you be my friend and give me strength after I am married?"

Now that Mr. Rochester confirmed that he did indeed plan to marry, I forced myself to hold back my tears. "I always try to be useful, sir, but you won't have any need of my services once you are married. I'm certain Miss Ingram will send Adele away to school."

I turned away from my master and quickly hurried toward the house, leaving him alone in the garden. I was nearing the front door to the house just as a small carriage drove up.

"Oh, Robert!" I cried, recognizing one of the Reed servants I had known at Gateshead. "What on earth are you doing here?"

"I've been sent here at my mistress's request, Miss Jane. There's been real trouble back at Gateshead. Mr. John died a week ago in London—suicide, they say. He had been wasting all of Mrs. Reed's money for years, gambling and running with the worst sort of ruffians.

When Mrs. Reed finally refused to give him another cent, they say he killed himself."

"How did Mrs. Reed take the news?"

"Her health has been bad for some years, Miss Jane, and the fear of poverty has made her worse. She had a stroke upon learning of John's death, but two days ago she was finally able to talk. What was so surprising, Miss, was that all she kept saying was, 'Jane, Jane, bring Jane here.' Can you return with me tomorrow morning, Miss?"

"Let me see if I can arrange that, Robert."

Once I had introduced Robert to Mrs. Fairfax, who promised to put him up for the night, I went in search of Mr. Rochester.

I found him in the billiard room with Miss Ingram and the other guests. She was the first to see me enter and she sneered, "What can that creature want now?"

Mr. Rochester turned and saw me. "What is it, Jane?"

"I need to take a week or two off, sir," I replied.

"Gateshead Is a Hundred Miles Away."

"What for?" he asked.

"To see Mrs. Reed, my uncle's wife, at Gateshead. She is quite ill."

"But you said you had no relations. Besides, Gateshead is a hundred miles away. And what concern is her health to you?" He was scowling now.

"She had a stroke after learning of her son's death. And even though she sent me away as a child, she told her daughters that she wants to see me now," I said.

"What good can you do for her? She'll probably be dead before you get there." The scowl deepened.

"Sir, if this was one of her last wishes, I must honor it," I insisted.

"Then promise me that you shall return."

"I promise." I turned and went to get ready for this most unexpected journey.

Mrs. Reed Is Awake.

CHAPTER 11

A Marriage Proposal

I left the following morning with Robert for Gateshead. Bessie was delighted to see me, but my cousins Eliza and Georgiana were as unfriendly as they had been when I lived there years before.

When they refused to tell their mother that I had arrived, I reminded them that it was she who had sent for me. I told Bessie to announce me.

A few minutes later, Bessie came downstairs and said, "Mrs. Reed is awake. Please follow me."

As I entered the room where I had received so many scoldings and punishments growing up, I felt no hatred toward the woman lying in the bed. Now it was pity. I truly wanted only to forgive and forget. I bent over the bed and gently kissed her cheek.

She glared at me and turned her face away. I sat down in a chair beside the bed and spoke softly. "It is Jane Eyre, Aunt Reed. You sent for me."

She turned to me with a dazed look in her eyes. "Oh, that child," she said as if speaking of someone else. "She was so evil. I hated her. I was glad to send her away. And when typhus broke out at Lowood, she didn't die, but I said she did. I wish she had died."

I could see that she was delirious, possibly even out of her mind as she continued. "My son John wasted all my money and now threatens to kill himself if I don't give him more."

Then, as if another person, one in her right mind, took over her body, she asked, "Is it you, Jane Eyre? I sent for you because I know I am near death. I need to confess two wrongs I did to you. First, I broke my promise to raise you as my own child.

"Second, I received a letter three years ago from John Eyre, your uncle. He was living in Spain, and wanted you to come to live with him. But I still felt deep hatred toward you."

"Please, Aunt Reed, don't excite yourself," I pleaded.

"No, let me finish," she said weakly. "I needed to take revenge on you. I didn't want you to have a comfortable life, which I knew you would have with your uncle, who had become quite wealthy. So, I wrote to him and told him you had died of typhus at Lowood."

"You are getting too upset, Aunt Reed. I forgive you. Now try to get some rest. We will talk more tomorrow."

That tomorrow never came, for that very night, Aunt Reed died. Neither of her daughters shed a tear. Nor did I.

Eliza and Georgiana pleaded with me to stay with them for several weeks after their mother's funeral, which I did. They were quite friendly to me, which was a great surprise to me. Georgiana was preparing to move to London.

I Chanced to Meet Him.

She hoped for a very active social life, while Eliza was going to a convent in France to become a nun.

I was happy to return to Thornfield for whatever time I had left with Adele before she was sent off to school. Mrs. Fairfax told me that Mr. Rochester had gone to London to make plans for his wedding, which was expected to take place shortly.

After I had put Adele to bed one evening, I was walking in the garden when I chanced to meet him.

He looked at me with a strange expression. "You have become quite fond of Thornfield and Adele and Mrs. Fairfax, haven't you, Jane?" he asked.

"Yes, sir."

"And you would be sad to leave all of them?"

"Yes, if I'm ordered to do so, sir," I said.

"Well, I am giving you that order now. Remember, Jane, it was you who said that if I married Miss Ingram, it would be better if you found another job and Adele were sent away to school."

It Started to Rain.

"Of course, sir," I whispered, trying not to let him see the tears that were ready to fall. It started to rain, as if heaven itself was in sympathy with me.

"I hope to be married in a month, and sadly, I shall never see you again. That troubles me greatly, but once you find a new position, you will forget all about me."

"I will never forget you, sir." I could no longer hold back my tears. The love I felt seemed to fill every tear that left my eyes. "I am terrified that I must leave you forever," I sobbed.

"But why must you?" he asked.

"Because of your bride," I sobbed.

"Bride? I have no bride," he replied.

"But you will soon, sir, and I am not a machine without feelings. If God had gifted me with beauty and wealth, such as Miss Ingram has, perhaps you would not find it so easy to let me go."

I had finally said it! I had finally confessed my love to Edward Rochester.

"Oh, Jane, my little Jane," he whispered

gently as he took me in his arms and kissed me.

"No, sir," I protested, pulling away. "You are practically a married man, married to a woman who is not as good as you, a woman you do not truly love."

As I struggled to get out of his arms, he spoke gently. "Stop it, Jane. It is you I want to marry, not Blanche Ingram."

"But why did you tell me you're marrying Blanche?" I argued. "You are making fun of me."

"No, Jane, I am not. Nor am I in love with Blanche Ingram who certainly doesn't love me. But I had to hear from your own lips how you felt about me."

"But I have no money and I am so plain-looking. How could you want to marry me?"

"Because I love you. I swear because you are the truest creature in the world. I shall never let you go."

"Oh, you have made my dreams come true," I sobbed, but happily now.

At that moment, thunder crashed and lightning flashed. The rain rushed down on us.

We hurried back to the house. Our tears of joy mixed with the raindrops falling on our faces.

As Edward took me in his arms to kiss me goodnight, I saw Mrs. Fairfax coming down the stairs, frowning as she saw us embrace.

I will explain to her in the morning, I said to myself as I hurried to my room.

Once there, I fell onto my bed, filled with joy at the thought of my life to come.

"Good Morning, Edward."

CHAPTER 12

A Terrible Secret Revealed

Edward canceled Adele's lessons the following morning. He sent for me to join him in the dining room.

"Good morning, sir," I said as I entered.

"Sir? Come now, Jane Eyre. You're soon to be Jane Rochester, in four weeks to be exact. I do have a first name, you know."

"Yes. Good morning, Edward." I blushed at my first use of his name.

"Now that that's settled, let me tell you what I have planned. I wrote to my banker in London who holds in his vault all the Rochester family jewels, which will be yours."

"I Will Give You Anything, Jane."

"No, Edward. Jewels are strange to Jane Eyre. I am not a beauty. I am not meant for jewels. I am a simple, plain-looking governess."

"You are a beauty in my eyes and you will wear jewels and satins and laces," Edward insisted.

"No, Edward. Then I won't be the Jane Eyre you fell in love with. I will not wear them."

"We'll talk about that later. Let me go on. We will be married in four weeks at the church just outside Thornfield's gates. Then we will travel to France and Italy. For the first time, I will go there in joy and not as an escape from Thornfield."

"Oh, my dear Edward, jewels and clothes and travel to foreign lands are generous of you, but I have only one request."

"Anything. I will give you anything, Jane."

"It is only an answer to a question that I wish from you."

"Is that all!" he said, laughing. "Then ask anything."

"Edward, why did you try so hard to make me believe you wanted to marry Blanche Ingram?"

"Because I wanted you to show that you were as much in love with me as I was with you. Making you jealous was the best way to get you to show it."

"But didn't you consider Miss Ingram's feelings? After all, she must feel terribly deserted."

"Actually, it was quite the opposite. She deserted me when she learned that I wasn't as wealthy as she thought. She wasn't in love with me, not the way you are, dear Jane."

"Yes, Edward, I love you more than my words can say. But one more thing. Please tell Mrs. Fairfax of our plans. She saw us kiss last night and she was not as friendly to me this morning as she usually is."

"I shall speak to her now while you go out to the carriage. We are going to Millcote to buy you some clothes and you will not refuse to go."

I insisted that Edward let me continue being Adele's governess until I became his wife. He wasn't happy about it, but I insisted and he let me have my way.

I wrote my uncle in Spain, explaining that I was still alive and about to be married. I wanted him to know of my good fortune in being settled in life.

The four weeks passed quickly. Two days before our wedding, my trunks were packed and ready to be shipped to London. How I looked lovingly at the name Jane Rochester printed on them. In my closet hung a pearl white satin gown and veil…my wedding dress.

Edward had gone off to settle some business before we left on our honeymoon.

I had spent a very difficult night. I was so anxious for his return that I paced back and forth in the driveway, eager to meet him. As the hours passed, I became more and more alarmed that some disaster had occurred.

Finally, I heard the tramp of hooves and Pilot's barks. Then Edward appeared.

"Oh, my darling," I sobbed. "I thought you would never come. I've been so worried."

"Is anything wrong, my dear? Your hands and cheeks are burning hot," he said.

My New Name

Once we were seated by the fire in the library, I explained. "Edward, I had a terrible dream last night. You were gone and I really couldn't talk to Mrs. Fairfax about it."

"Well, I'm here now, dear Jane, and you will never have such dreams again," Edward said gently. "We will talk of them now, then forget them."

"Edward, I dreamt that Thornfield was in ruins, with only a few walls still standing. I wandered alone, calling out for you and Adele, for Mrs. Fairfax and the servants. But no one was there. At one point, I lost my footing and fell. That woke me."

"Surely, Jane, it was nothing but a bad dream. Look around you. Everything in the house is fine."

"But that isn't all, Edward. When I opened my eyes, a candle was burning on my dressing table. The door to my closet was open, and suddenly, a figure came out. It was a large woman with thick, black hair and red eyes. She was wearing something white, a gown or a sheet, I don't know what. But she was holding my wedding veil. She put the veil on her head. Then she pulled it off and tore it in two, and trampled it under her feet.

"I was frozen with fear, Edward, and for only the second time in my life, I lost consciousness."

"And who was there when you woke?"

"No one. I didn't tell anyone. I waited for you. Please, Edward—tell me who or what this woman is."

"Jane, Jane, it was part of your nightmare."

"No, Edward, it wasn't! That thing was real. How I wish to God it were a nightmare! And my torn veil on the floor this morning, how do you explain that?"

Edward took me in his arms. "Thank God only the veil was harmed, not you. Perhaps it was Grace Poole after all."

"Then why do you keep her here?" I cried. By now, I was becoming hysterical.

"Trust me, Jane. After we are married, I will explain it all. In the meantime, sleep in the nursery tonight and dream of our love."

I did as he asked, but my excitement over my wedding day kept me from sleeping too many hours. I awoke, eager to greet my groom downstairs. I pinned a white lace handkerchief on my head to replace the torn wedding veil.

"You are my beautiful Jane," he said. He hurried me through the door and down the driveway to the church. As we passed the churchyard, I noticed two strangers looking at the headstones, but I didn't think it important enough to point them out to Edward. He was too eager to get inside.

The priest was waiting at the altar. Out of the corner of my eye, I saw the two men were now inside the church.

The ceremony began. The priest came to the part where he asked if anyone knew "why these two people shouldn't be legally married in the eyes of God." He paused, as is the custom. Then he went on. "Will you, Edward Rochester, have this woman, Jane Eyre, for your wedded wife?"

Suddenly, from behind us came a man's

"The Marriage Cannot Go On."

solemn voice. "The marriage cannot go on."

Edward turned white, but commanded the priest to proceed.

"I cannot proceed until I know whether there is any truth to this person's words," said the priest.

The man came forward and calmly said, "Mr. Edward Rochester already has a wife."

I looked up into Edward's face, now gone white, as he drew me tightly against him and demanded of the man, "Who are you?"

"My name is Briggs. I'm an attorney from London. I have in my possession a legal document, which proves that you, Edward Rochester of Thornfield Hall, married a woman named Bertha Mason in Jamaica. This document was signed by her brother, Richard Mason, and legally witnessed. He claims that his sister is alive."

At hearing the name Richard Mason, Edward clenched his teeth. His body shook with rage. Then the second stranger stepped forward from the shadows and stood beside

Briggs. It was the same Richard Mason who had been at Thornfield only a few months ago!

The priest was still doubtful. "I have been in this neighborhood for many years and I never heard of a Mrs. Rochester at Thornfield."

"No!" shouted Edward. "I made certain that no one would know about her. It is true that I married Bertha Mason fifteen years ago. But she is mad, a lunatic! Her family has three generations of madness to prove it. I was tricked into marrying her by her family and my father. But let me show you the truth of my words. All of you, come with me to Thornfield Hall.

"There will be no wedding today, but you must know that Jane had no knowledge of this woman. She did not know she was being deceived into marriage with a man who already had a wife."

With Edward half-dragging me and the two men and the priest behind us, we hurried to Thornfield. Mrs. Fairfax and the servants were waiting, prepared to congratulate us,

The Priest Was Still Doubtful.

only to have Edward rush past them.

"Out of my way, everyone!" he shouted as we climbed the stairs. Once inside the third-floor bedroom, he lifted the tapestry covering the iron door and snarled to Mason, "Surely you remember this place, Richard. This is where she bit and stabbed you."

Edward unlocked the door and opened it. Grace Poole was cooking something in the fire-place. In a dark corner, a figure was running backward and forward on all fours, growling like a wild animal.

"Good day, Miss Poole," Edward said, "how is your patient today?"

A fierce cry from the creature's mouth filled the room as it stood up on its two legs.

"Be careful, sir," warned Grace. "I never know if she is hiding a knife in her gown."

The creature screamed. She pushed aside the long hair covering her eyes in order to see her visitors.

"That face!" I gasped. "She was the crea-ture in my room two nights ago!"

"That Face!" I Gasped.

Edward pulled me behind him, away from the crazy woman, just as she sprang at him. She grabbed his throat and bit into his cheek. He struggled with her but would not actually strike her.

Finally, after several minutes of her fierce yells and thrusts of her body, he pinned her arms behind her and, with Grace's help, they tied her to a chair.

Once Bertha was subdued, Edward turned to everyone. "That is my wife. That is the love I get from my marriage, all that I have ever had for fifteen years. Can you blame me for wishing to have this wonderful young woman, Jane Eyre, who is warm and gentle and knows what love is?"

Edward's voice turned even colder. "Now, leave, all of you. I must lock up my wife."

On the way down the stairs, Mr. Briggs further explained to me, "Miss Eyre, your uncle will be glad to hear you are alive and safe, that is, if he is still alive. He has been quite ill, but I will send him word with Mr. Mason, who is on his way to Spain."

"I don't understand, Mr. Briggs. What do you have to do with my uncle?" I asked.

"I do not, but Mr. Mason has been doing business with your uncle for some years. When Mr. Eyre received your letter announcing your upcoming marriage to Mr. Rochester, Mr. Mason just happened to be in your uncle's office. Of course, Mr. Mason immediately told your uncle of the situation with the Rochester family. Since your uncle was ill and getting worse, he couldn't make the trip to England himself to save you from the horrible fate of a false marriage, so he had Mr. Mason refer the matter to my law office."

The two men left Thornfield immediately after this conversation. I rushed up to my room and locked myself in. I took off my wedding dress and lay down across my bed to think. My hopes and dreams were dead. I could not reach out to Edward to comfort me…not now…not ever!

I must leave Thornfield, I told myself. How or where to go, I didn't know. But I had to

Even Though I Fought It

leave immediately. Still, even though I fought it, my exhausted body fell into a deep sleep.

But how I was able to sleep, I never shall know. Yet sleep I did, deeply and quietly, without disturbing dreams. But what dream, if indeed one came, could rival the horror and the drama of what I had actually been through?

Reader, never had I imagined such a day ever to occur in the life of anyone, let alone such a one as myself. Never had I expected to find the love I had with Edward, but once having secured such joy, I had not thought to lose it so quickly, so completely.

My beautiful new life was over before it had begun. What would happen to Jane Eyre now?

"I Have Been Here for Hours."

CHAPTER 13

Edward Rochester's Unhappy Life

Late that afternoon, I finally raised my head off the bed. I was still convinced that I had to leave Thornfield, but was I strong enough to leave Edward?

I tried to sit up, but found my head spinning. I got to my feet and stumbled to the door. As I opened it, my legs went limp under me. But I didn't fall. Edward, who was just outside my door, caught me.

"I have been here for hours, listening for a sob or some movement," he explained. "Five minutes more and I would have broken down the door. I was hoping you'd be crying after all that happened, but your eyes are dry. Have you no feeling at all for me? Can you ever forgive me?"

Reader, I forgave him that very moment, not in words, but in my heart. But all I could say to him was, "I am tired and ill, Edward. Please, I need some water."

Edward carried me down to the library. After he set me down in his chair, he poured me some water and brought me a bit to eat.

He bent down to kiss me, but I turned away. "You have a wife, Edward. Kissing me is not proper. I feel that living here in your house as Adele's governess is not proper either. I must leave and you must hire a new governess."

"I should never have brought you here, Jane," he said sadly. "Adele will be sent off to school. I cannot put that maniac Bertha anywhere else, but you and I can leave here, Jane. We can be together at my villa in France. There, we can have a happy life."

I shook my head. "No, Edward. Please sit down and stop pacing the floor." I finally let my

I Forgave Him That Moment.

tears fall. Edward tried to take me in his arms, but I drew back. "Listen, please, Edward. I do love you, now more than ever. But this is the last time I will ever say it, for I must leave you, leave Adele and leave Thornfield. I must begin a whole new life elsewhere."

"Jane, please, please listen for only a few minutes," he pleaded. "When I say I am not married, I must explain to you why. Please, just a few minutes."

"I will listen to you for hours, sir, if you need to talk."

"You know from Mrs. Fairfax that I had an older brother, Rowland. We were the sons of a greedy man. He who refused to divide his estate between us and left it all to Rowland. But he wouldn't have a son of his–me–be known as a poor man. He arranged a wealthy marriage for me with the daughter of an old business partner of his in Jamaica.

"I wasn't told that her family would be giving 30,000 pounds to my father and brother as the money for her dowry; I was only told that she was beautiful. So, at the age of twenty-two, I was sent to Jamaica. Bertha and I spent time together only at parties or with her family, never alone. I never really knew her, never really spoke to her. I was attracted by her beauty, stupid blockhead that I was. So I married her, only to discover my mistake soon afterwards.

"The family said her mother was dead, but I discovered she was in a lunatic asylum, along with a younger brother. My father and brother both knew this family history, but they thought only of the 30,000 pounds, and so in their greed, they plotted against me.

"I quickly learned that my so-called wife could not even hold a conversation with me, could not run a household, had a violent and unreasonable temper, and gave crazy orders to the servants. She did other things too terrible for me to repeat to you, Jane.

"I lived with her in Jamaica for four years and suffered incredibly hideous agonies. Yet, I couldn't be cruel to her.

"It wasn't her fault. During these years,

both Rowland and my father died. So, I became a very wealthy man and inherited Thornfield Hall. Even after the best doctors pronounced Bertha mad, I could do nothing. At the age of twenty-six, I was bound to her for life. I was so desperate, I even considered killing myself.

"Then I thought that if I returned to England and took her with me, no one would know I had a maniac monster for a wife. I could hire someone to care for her at Thornfield in secrecy, and I could live my life traveling, as I have been doing all these years.

"Bertha has lived for ten years in that den on the third floor. I hired Grace Poole to care for her. Only Grace and Dr. Carter, who treated Mason, know about Bertha.

"Bertha is cunning and vicious. Sometimes she manages to fool Grace. She has stolen the key to her room and has hidden knives. Yes, she did try to burn me in my bed and yes, she paid that ghastly visit to you and tore your wedding veil, and yes, only this very morning she flew at my throat to try to get to you.

"I truly believed I had a right to find a good woman to love and be happy with, one who could understand the burden I'm cursed with. I searched all over the world for ten long years, then I found you, my darling Jane.

"I know it was wrong not to tell you. I was a coward, but I couldn't afford to lose you and lose all the goodness and sweetness you brought into my life. Please, Jane, stay with me."

Then came the most difficult words I have ever said. "No, Edward, I cannot. You must go on with your life. You will soon forget me, but please, my dearest, know that I will never forget you."

"Never have I met anyone so frail, yet so immovable! Has nothing I've said changed your mind?" he pleaded.

"No, sir. I am going. I must." I stood up.

"Oh, Jane, my hope, my love, my life!"

He turned away from me.

"I Am Going. I Must."

CHAPTER 14

Safety at Moor House

That night, I lay down with my clothes on and stared at the ceiling until dawn came. I rose and gathered a few pieces of clothing and my purse containing twenty shillings, all the money I had in the world. I pinned on my shawl and carried my shoes as I tiptoed out of my room.

"Good-bye, kind Mrs. Fairfax," I whispered as I passed her door.

"Good-bye, dear little Adele," I sobbed as I glanced into the nursery. "How I wish I could give you one last kiss."

My heart stopped as I hesitated outside

Edward's door.

I heard him pacing the floor. I knew all I needed to do was open his door, and find love and happiness. My hand reached out for the doorknob, but I pulled my hand back and made my way down the stairs to the kitchen door. I stopped only to take some bread and water.

Minutes later, I was outside the gates of Thornfield. I was heading away from the only place where I had known true happiness.

I took the road going in the opposite direction from the familiar town of Millcote. It was a road I had never traveled before. I hated myself for hurting Edward, but I couldn't turn back. I walked for miles, all day and into the night, before I fell to my knees from exhaustion and grief.

A coach came down the road, going in the same direction I was. I didn't have enough money to go as far as it was headed, but I gave the driver my entire twenty shillings to take me as far as the money would go. Once I was seated in the empty coach, I finally let my tears flow.

I rode for two days, eating only the bread and drinking the water I had with me. The coach dropped me off at a crossroads, with no town in sight.

Night found me in the road looking at the land all around. It was covered in swampy bogs and moors, where very little grew. There were no people on the road and no houses I could see in any direction. I walked into the moor until I could walk no longer. I saw a large rock with a cutout ledge. I could sleep under that ledge and have some protection from the weather.

For days I wandered, how many I cannot remember. I slept under trees with nothing to eat and only drops of water from the morning dew to drink. I staggered through Whitcross and other villages where I tried to trade my gloves and my handkerchief for food, but no one wanted them.

I looked for any kind of work at several houses, but no one would have me. I was beginning to look like a beggar.

I Tried to Trade for Food.

I continued walking. I went into the woods for shelter from a fierce night wind that was moaning all around me. Rain began to fall, getting heavier with each step I took, drenching me completely.

I stumbled and fell in the mud. I got up and tried to walk toward a dim light that seemed to stay in one spot. As I came closer to it, I prayed that my eyes weren't playing tricks on me.

Step by step, I approached the light. It was coming from an ivy-covered cottage. I fell to my knees and peered into the low candlelit window.

Two young ladies, both in black mourning dresses, sat reading aloud. A strange language reached my ears. I was later to learn that they were teaching themselves to speak German. When they switched to English, I heard one of them ask the other, "Do you know when St. John will be home?"

"By ten, I hope, for the rain is starting to come down very hard," answered the other.

Just then, an elderly woman entered the room wiping her eyes on her apron. "It is sad to go into his room now," she sobbed. "But I know he's in a better place. I'm just glad that your father had a quiet death."

I was desperate for food and warmth after starving for so many days outdoors. I knocked weakly at the door.

The elderly woman, a housekeeper, I assumed, answered my knock. "What do you want?" she asked, leaning out the door.

"I am a stranger. Please, may I speak to your mistresses? I need a night's shelter in a barn or anywhere, and a bit of bread to eat."

"I'll give you some bread and a penny, but we do not take in strangers."

"Please, please!" I pleaded. "I have no strength to go on. Don't shut the door. I'll die out here!"

"I must shut it. The rain is coming in. Now move away!" She slammed the door shut.

I sank to the ground and sobbed out loud, "All I can do is die here and wait for God to take me."

Then from above me came a voice. "All beings must die, but not here and not because of needing food and shelter." Then the man whose voice it was knocked hard on the door.

"Who is speaking?" I asked, terrified.

The voice called out, "Hannah, open the door. It is I, St. John."

The door opened and Hannah said, "Come in quickly. Your sisters have been worried about you. And there's been a beggar woman here. Oh, she's still here. Move off, young woman!"

"Hush, Hannah," said the man called St. John. "Let her into the house so that I may hear her story."

With the young man helping me, I stumbled into the warm, bright kitchen and collapsed into a chair.

One sister, Diana, tore some bread into pieces, dipped it into warm milk and put it to my lips. In a sweet, calming voice, she said, "Try to eat."

"Do try," said the other sister, Mary, as she took off my soaking wet bonnet and shawl.

"Let Her into the House."

"Feed her slowly," said the brother, St. John. "Not too much at first."

I felt some strength returning and I was able to speak. "My name is Jane, Jane Elliott," I said, using a false name so as not to be discovered.

"And what happened to you, Miss Elliott?" asked St. John.

"I cannot give you any details tonight," I pleaded. "I am too weak to move or speak much."

The brother and sisters whispered among themselves, then nodded to each other. The two ladies helped me up a staircase, took off the rest of my dripping wet clothes and put me into a warm, dry bed.

I recall thanking them and thanking God. And for the first time in so many days, I slept joyously.

I remember little of the next three days and nights. I lay in that small bed in that small room, as motionless as if I were part of the bed itself. I heard whispering when Diana and Mary came in, but saw a frowning face when

They Helped Me Up a Staircase.

Hannah bent over me.

By the fourth day, I was able to sit up and eat some porridge and toast. Later, I felt my strength returning. I noticed that my muddy clothes had been washed clean and were neatly folded.

I got dressed but I had to rest for several minutes after I put on each garment. My clothes hung on my body from all the weight I had lost during these terrible days. Still, I tried to look neat as I could as I slowly made my way down a stone staircase and into the kitchen.

Hannah was baking bread. She even managed a smile for me. She was finally convinced that I was not a beggar, and we were soon chatting like old friends. Hannah told me she had been with the Rivers family for thirty years and had helped raise St. John, Diana and Mary. Their father had lived in this house and had died just three weeks earlier.

Moors End, as the area was called, had been in the Rivers family for 200 years. Diana and Mary worked as governesses for wealthy

Chatting Like Old Friends.

families in London and returned here on visits to their father. St. John, who was a parson in a village several miles away, lived at the parsonage at his church. All three were here for their father's funeral and for the mourning period following it.

Diana, Mary and St. John came in from a walk and joined us in the kitchen for tea. It was then that St. John told me that I had been running a high fever for three days and hadn't been able to eat anything.

"I'm certain that I will not be an expense for you much longer," I said softly.

"Then just tell us how we can reach your family or friends," said St. John, "and we can write to them to come get you."

"That is not possible, sir," I replied. "I have no home, no family and no friends." My answer stunned them, but I went on. "I want to find work to support myself. I will never forget how you saved me from death. I cannot give you details of my recent life, only that it was necessary for me to leave my job, a happy one,

I Was Happy.

some days before I came here. Leaving was not my fault, and I had to spend what little money I had on a coach that took me to a crossroads ten miles from Whitcross."

"But that is miles away from here!" cried Diana.

"And you are still weak, Miss Elliott," Mary said.

I was startled when I heard the false name I had given them. "Elliott is not my real name, but for now I must ask you not to question why I have chosen to use an alias. Please don't send me back out, penniless. I can work. I can sew or clean or be a servant. I will work at anything."

"You shall stay here, Jane, until you are well," stated Diana firmly.

"Yes," added Mary. "You must stay with us."

Reader, I was happy. Moor House, and the women inside it, gave me warmth and comfort I thought I might never have known again.

Jane Eyre, Jane Elliot, whoever—I would survive and make my way somehow.

CHAPTER 15

A New Family

My days at Moor House became quite pleasant as I began to get well. Diana, Mary and I spent hours talking and reading together and taking walks out on the moor, enjoying nature.

The closeness that grew between the girls and myself did not, however, include their brother. St. John was busy visiting the sick and poor in his parish and didn't spend much time at Moor House.

A month passed. Soon Mary and Diana had to return to their jobs. I, too, had to find a job for myself. I took the opportunity to speak

I Spoke to St. John.

to St. John on his next visit to Moor House. "Sir, your sisters are leaving in three days. I wondered if you had heard of any position for me."

"Yes, I have," he replied. "It is a position with me in my parish. I have set up a school for the poor local boys. Now I wish to open such a school for the girls. I have rented a cottage for a teacher next to the school. But we are a poor parish, and can only offer thirty pounds year."

St. John spoke quickly, as if trying to get the words out of his mouth before I refused. But I simply smiled and said, "Thank you, Mr. Rivers. I accept it with all my heart."

Yet another sadness reached the Rivers family the next day. St. John entered the house and announced coldly, "Our Uncle John is dead." He tossed a letter on the table for his sisters to read.

When I looked at the girls and saw no sign of tears, I was bewildered.

But Diana explained, "Please don't think we are uncaring, Jane, but we have never seen this uncle. He was our mother's brother, but we didn't know him at all. He and our father had a fight many years ago over some bad investments that lost a great deal of money for our family. As a result, they stopped talking.

"Years later, Uncle John made a fortune. Since he never married, his only relative was one other niece besides Mary and me, and no other nephews besides St. John. I suppose because our father and Uncle John never made up, he left his fortune to this other niece."

We never discussed this lost inheritance any further, for the girls were very busy packing. The following day everyone left. Mary and Diana went back to London. St. John returned to the parsonage, along with Hannah and me.

Five weeks ago, I was an outcast and nearly a beggar. Now I had a neat little two-room cottage that was more than enough for my needs. Through the kindness of Diana and Mary, I had clothing and some paints and paper to continue my artwork.

A School for Girls

Of the twenty girls in my school, only three knew how to read and none could write. Some did not really want to learn, while others were eager to do so. So here I was, a village schoolteacher, earning my own living.

Yet as busy as I was, not a day passed by without my thinking about Edward and what despair he must have felt at finding me gone.

As the days wore on, I became even busier with my work. I was welcomed in many homes with kindness and gratitude. But when my chores were done and hours of reading or painting were over, I would fall asleep still thinking about Edward Rochester.

St. John had not been to my school during my first month there, so it came as a surprise when he knocked at my cottage door one afternoon.

For someone who had always been so cold, he offered me kind words. "I am most pleased with your success at the school. I admire talent and hard work." Then he added, "You are an energetic woman in spite of some

He Pulled One from the Pile.

hurt from your past."

"Because I have not talked about my past doesn't mean I had been hurt," I replied.

"But I can see some hurt in your paintings," he said. He picked up some of my sketches from the kitchen table.

He began looking through them. Suddenly he pulled one from the pile and stared at the bottom right corner. He turned to me with a strange, puzzled expression on his face.

"What is the matter, St. John?" I asked.

"Nothing," he quickly replied. Then with an abrupt "Good afternoon," he left the house.

I fastened the door tightly and made certain that all the windows were closed because it was beginning to snow. The snow fell heavily that night and continued into the next day and evening. So, I was surprised to see St. John at my door that night, his cloak all covered in snow.

"Is anything wrong?" I asked, worried that something might have happened to one of my pupils.

"No, no, do not be upset," he said as he stepped through the doorway. "I must talk to you."

"Of course, St. John. Come sit by the fire."

"I shall tell you a story which you may already know. Twenty years ago, a poor curate and rich man's daughter fell in love. Against the wishes of her family, they married. Before two years had passed, they both died and left an infant daughter. The baby was taken in by the mother's brother, who died within a few years. After his death—and now I shall use names—his widow, Mrs. Reed of Gateshead…Oh, Jane, you jumped. Are you all right?

"Mrs. Reed kept the orphan until she was ten then sent her off to Lowood School.

"She was a talented student and popular teacher. She left Lowood to become a governess for a Mr. Edward Rochester."

I tried to interrupt St. John, but he didn't let me.

"Wait! I'm almost finished. I don't know this Mr. Rochester, but I am told he wanted to marry this girl, but on their wedding day she dis-

I Tried to Interrupt.

covered he had a wife, a lunatic. The governess ran away the following day while everyone in the house was asleep. Although Mr. Rochester searched everywhere for her, he never found her. He put notices in all the newspapers and hired private investigators to search for her, but there was no trace of this governess."

"How did you learn all this?" I demanded.

"From an attorney named Briggs."

"And since you know so much, what can you tell me of Mr. Rochester? How is he? Where is he?" I demanded

"I know nothing of Mr. Rochester. But why don't you ask me the name of the governess? It seems to be urgent that she is found."

I ignored St. John's question and replied with one of my own. "Did you or Mr. Briggs write to Mr. Rochester?"

"Briggs did, but his letter was answered by a Mrs. Alice Fairfax."

My thoughts went to my poor dear master and to the suffering he must have gone through. He must have left England, I thought to myself, and that is the reason why Mrs. Fairfax answered the letter.

St. John continued. "And just to let you know, Jane, how I came to my suspicions, it was this." And he went to the pile of drawings he had admired the day before and pulled out one in particular. It was a sketch I had done of Edward. In the bottom right corner was the artist's signature, in my own handwriting: Jane Eyre. It was something I must have done without thinking.

"But why would this name have any meaning for you?" I asked.

"Briggs wrote me about a Jane Eyre. I only knew a Jane Elliott."

"All right, St. John, so you know. Where is Mr. Briggs? He must know of Mr. Rochester."

"Jane, aren't you curious about why Mr. Briggs has been so interested in finding you?"

"Well, what did he want?" I asked without much curiosity.

"Merely to tell you that your uncle, John Eyre, had died in Spain and left you his fortune."

The Family Connection!

"What? I? Rich?" I was stunned. In one moment was I to be raised from poverty to wealth and independence?

As St. John got up to leave, a sudden thought struck me. I grabbed hold of his arm and demanded, "Why would Mr. Briggs write to you about me? And how did he even know you? And how could he imagine that someone living in such an out-of-the-way village could help him locate me?"

"I'll tell you another time," he said, pulling his arm away.

"No, now!" I shouted as I ran to the door and blocked his way. "You must tell me now."

"Well, you'll know one day anyway, so I guess I might as well tell you now. You are Jane Eyre, aren't you?"

"Of course! You already know that."

"But what you don't know is that my full name is St. John Eyre Rivers. My mother was an Eyre."

I suddenly realized the full family connection! "Yes, St. John," I cried. "My mother, Jane

Reed, became Jane Reed Eyre when she married my father, Richard Eyre. My mother's brother was the Uncle Reed who took me in."

"Yes, Jane," said St. John. "Your father had a sister and a brother. His sister married into the Rivers family and was my mother. His brother was John Eyre, a merchant who never married."

"So, where does Mr. Briggs fit into all this?" I asked.

"Mr. Briggs was John Eyre's attorney. He notified us when you were at Moor House our uncle, John Eyre had died and left his fortune to the daughter of his brother, Richard. Briggs asked if we knew anything of her. He had been unable to locate her. Then the name signed on your drawing gave me my answer. Your father was my mother's brother."

"Then you and Diana and Mary are my cousins!" I exclaimed joyfully. "Oh, I have a family and to have a family is true wealth, not the kind of wealth measured by our uncle's money! Oh, I am so happy!"

"How can you say the money is not important, Jane?" he asked.

"Because until this moment, I had no family and now I have three cousins. I will divide my inheritance equally among the four of us. Please, St. John, write to Diana and Mary. Have them come home and we shall all collect our inheritance. They do not have to work."

"Jane, please, you are confused. You've become too excited. You cannot imagine what this fortune will do for your life."

"And you, St. John, cannot imagine the yearning I have had for a family and for love."

"But, Jane, we will be a family anyway, without the money," were his kind words.

"I won't have Diana and Mary slaving in the homes of wealthy strangers, and I know you will use your share to help your parishioners," I said.

My heart overflowing with joy, I sent St. John home.

Diana and Mary protested my giving them part of the money. I insisted and remained firm. They finally gave in, and all the legal arrangements were made.

Everything was accomplished by Christmas, and I moved back into Moor House with Hannah to help. I bought new furniture, carpets and curtains. Hannah and I prepared for Mary and Diana's homecoming. They were overjoyed at seeing me and the changes I had made. We soon settled into a pleasant and happy life together.

St. John, however, showed no interest in anything but his work. He spoke only of his plans to become a missionary and travel to India.

Perhaps, reader, you're thinking that with all my newfound happiness at finding a family, I had forgotten my dear Edward Rochester. Not for a moment. The wish to know what had become of him was with me every day.

I wrote to Mr. Briggs, but he had no information. I wrote to Mrs. Fairfax several times. When six months had passed without any word from her, I became very concerned.

On one occasion when we were alone, St. John asked me to go to India with him as a fellow missionary and as his wife. I couldn't dream of marrying him. I didn't love him and I knew he didn't love me.

The night before St. John was to leave, he tried one more time to convince me to go with him. From somewhere, I don't know where, I heard a voice—not St. John's voice—crying out, "Jane! Jane! Jane!"

It was a human voice and a beloved one. It was Edward Rochester's voice urgently calling to me in despair.

"I'm coming! Wait for me!" I cried as I flew to the door and looked outside. "Where are you?"

There was nothing but the blackness of night out on the moor.

I hurried up to my room. I knew what I must do the very next day. Never was I more anxious for daylight to come.

Rochester's Voice Was Calling to Me.

CHAPTER 16

Devastating Ruins!

I rose at dawn the following day. I put my room in order since I planned to be gone for several days. I had to find out what had become of my beloved Edward after not receiving any replies to the letters I had been sending for months and especially after hearing what I was certain was his voice the night before.

Diana and Mary didn't know the real reason I was going. I simply explained that I was seeking news of an old friend.

I made my way this time by carriage, not on foot—to the same crossroads where the coach had dropped me off a year ago.

A Blackened Ruin!

When the coach finally reached Millcote, I left my trunk at the inn and hired a carriage. I wanted to drive to Thornfield, but not directly up to the door. I preferred to cross the old, familiar field on foot before I had my first glimpse of the house.

I left the horse and carriage on the road. I crossed the field leading to Thornfield almost as quickly as I had when I'd run away a year ago. I looked forward to seeing Thornfield's majestic front, and even more so to seeing Edward's window, or even perhaps Edward himself!

How excited I was as I left the woods, only to come face to face with…a blackened ruin!

The walls of the house had tumbled down, leaving only a blackened shell. The windows had no panes. The chimneys had crashed down into piles of rocks. In between the rocks and stones, weeds grew everywhere. And all around this devastation was total silence. The silence of death! My heart froze with panic.

The blackness of the stones can only have

been the result of a terrible fire, I thought, my mind racing. But how did it start? Where were Mrs. Fairfax, the servants? Where was Edward?

As I wandered through the shattered walls and piles of rocks, I realized that the fire had not been recent. Mounds of rubbish and leaves had accumulated, and grass had grown between the fallen stones as well as the weeds. I wept silently for the beauty that had been destroyed, and I longed even more to know what had become of the owner of these ruins.

At that moment, I remembered the terrible nightmare I had had over a year ago. I had seen Thornfield in ruins, but Edward had comforted me at the time. Now, it seemed as if that nightmare had become a reality. But now there was no sign of Edward to comfort me.

I could find no answers here among the ruins, so I hurried to my carriage and returned to the inn at Millcote. Surely the innkeeper would know what had happened.

The Innkeeper Would Know.

"Yes, ma'am, I do," the innkeeper said in answer to my question. "There was a terrible fire last fall. It broke out in the middle of the night. None of the valuable furniture or possessions could be saved by the time the fire wagons arrived from the village."

"And does anyone know how it started?" I asked.

"Well, ma'am, you seem to be a stranger in these parts, so I will tell you what everyone around here knows. There was a crazy woman living in that house. It turned out that when Mr. Rochester was to be married to a young governess at Thornfield, this lunatic was found out to be his wife."

"But the fire," I interrupted, not wanting to hear my own tragedy retold, but desperate for news of Edward and the others.

"On this night last fall, she set fire to the room next to hers. Then she went downstairs and set fire to the bed in the governess's room, but the governess wasn't there anymore. She had run away two months earlier.

"Mr. Rochester searched the world over but never found her. He was never a wild man, but he became dangerous when he lost this young lady. He insisted on being completely alone. He sent the girl Adele off to school and gave Mrs. Fairfax a fine pension to go live with friends. Then he stopped seeing everyone he knew."

"Was Mr. Rochester at home when the fire occurred?"

"Oh, yes, ma'am. It was he who woke the servants and helped them to safety. And he even went back into the flames to get his mad wife out. But she had climbed out onto the roof, waving her arms and laughing hysterically. I was there and saw it with my own eyes."

"And what happened?" I could scarcely contain myself.

"Well, Mr. Rochester climbed out onto the roof after her and when he was about to grab her to pull her back inside, she pushed him away. She was a big, strong woman. The next minute, she jumped to her death."

"How terrible!" I gasped. "And Mr. Rochester?"

"Mr. Rochester climbed back inside, but everything was in flames. The stairs and walls crashed down on him. The firemen pulled him out from the ruins, but he was badly injured. One of his hands was crushed and he lost his sight in one eye. The other eye was badly damaged. So, he is blind and a cripple."

"And where is Mr. Rochester now?" My heart was racing so I could hardly speak.

"He's locked himself up like a hermit on his farm in Ferndean, about thirty miles from here."

"I must have a carriage and driver to take me to Ferndean immediately," I told him.

"It will be at the front door within minutes, ma'am," the innkeeper promised. But even minutes seemed like an eternity to me.

CHAPTER 17

Finding Edward Rochester

It was evening and raining when I finally reached Ferndean. I had to leave the carriage a mile away from the cottage. The woods were too thick for it to pass through so I walked the last mile alone on a path that led to a small, dark, dreary-looking house.

I stopped at the edge of the woods when I saw the front door open. A man stepped out slowly. I could still recognize the figure of my beloved Edward.

I caught my breath and dared not move. Of course, he couldn't see me, but I could see him well enough. His body was as straight as ever, but his face looked sadder than I could ever remember.

And, reader, you must know that I did not love him less because he was blind. I loved him all the more.

I saw him walk slowly and hesitantly, with his good right arm outstretched to feel his way in front of him. He seemed to ignore the rain as it came down on him.

When Edward finally groped his way back inside the house and closed the door, I waited for a few minutes. Then I approached and knocked lightly.

John's wife Mary, answered. "Is it really you, miss?" she gasped, as if she had seen a ghost.

I took her hand and patted it to calm her. We went into the kitchen where John was seated by the fire. When he saw me, his wrinkled face broke into a wide smile.

Just then, a bell rang from the parlor.

"I must bring the master some water," said Mary. "That's what he usually rings for at this

"So, He Is Blind."

A Man Stepped Out Slowly.

hour." And she placed the glass on a tray with two lit candles, explaining, "The master always requests candles even though he is blind."

"I will bring the tray in to him," I said, taking it from her.

My shaking hands caused half the water to spill, but I continued into the parlor. There, standing in front of the fire with his head leaning on the mantel, was my beloved Edward. Pilot was at his feet, and bounded up with a yelp when he saw me approaching.

"Give me the water, Mary," Edward said as he reached to take the glass I held out to him.

"Mary is in the kitchen," I said softly.

"Who are you?" he demanded. "Answer me! These worthless eyes do not let me see anything!"

"Pilot knows me, and so do Old John and Mary," I whispered.

"Good God!" he cried. "What madness has come over me?"

"It is not madness, sir. Your mind and your body are much too strong for madness," I said.

"Answer me!"

"Where are you? I must touch you to see if you are real." His hand came toward me and I caught it in mine.

"It is her fingers, her small, gentle fingers. "Is it really you, Jane?"

"Yes, Edward. Jane is here with you. I have come back and I will never leave you again." I put my arms around him and kissed him. "But if you do not wish me to live with you, Edward, I shall build my own house right next to yours. I am a rich woman now and quite independent, and I can do things on my own."

"Oh, my Jane, I am happy that you are rich and independent. But now you don't have to spend your life taking care of a blind man like me."

"Dear Edward, it is because I am independent that I can make my own choices," I replied. "And I choose to be with you, to walk with you, to read to you, to wait on you, and be eyes and hands to you."

"You must not spend your years being my nurse. I am certain I must be a ghastly sight, with scars from the fire and no useful hand on

We Sat by the Fire Talking.

one arm. I must be revolting to you."

"Foolish thoughts, sir. And here I thought you still had good judgment."

I managed to persuade Edward to sit down to dinner with me even though he protested that he barely ate anything. Afterwards, we sat by the fire talking. Edward wanted to know all that I had been doing since I'd left. He seemed grateful for each word I spoke, and if I hesitated, he would reach out for me to be sure I was still there. But I was not yet ready to tell him the full story of all my suffering.

When it was time for Old John to take him up to bed, Edward said to me, "I fear going to sleep tonight, only to wake tomorrow and find you gone."

"I am staying here with you, just as I have been staying with good people these last several months. But I will tell you that part of my story tomorrow."

I Greeted Him Cheerfully.

CHAPTER 18

True Happiness at Last

The following morning, I made certain that Old John had brought Edward down to breakfast before I joined him. How sad he looked, a strong man now so powerless!

I greeted him cheerfully as I kissed his cheek. "It is a bright, sunny morning, Edward, just perfect for a walk after breakfast."

His face took on a glow. "Then you have not vanished, my darling Jane. I can feel the sunshine just because you are near."

My eyes filled with tears, which I quickly dried so that Edward would not be concerned. We talked over breakfast, then went out walking in the open fields beyond the woods.

It was then that I told him the details of my life that past year. I didn't dwell on the days I had spent wandering on foot, with no food and with no money. I didn't tell him how I was close to death from starvation. Those details would have been too painful for him to bear.

"Dear Jane, if you had just told me how much you wanted to leave, I would have helped you. I would have given you money without expecting anything in return."

After I had told him of my time at Moor House and the cousins I'd discovered I had, he asked me, "And this St. John, did you like him?"

"He was a good man, sir. Of course I liked him."

"And was he a respectable man at least fifty years old?" he wanted to know.

"Oh, no. St. John was only twenty-nine and a very educated and intelligent man. A real gentleman and quite handsome." I saw that jealousy had really gotten hold of Edward, but I hoped it would pull him out of his depression and make him stop feeling sorry for himself.

After I had described St. John, Edward let go of my hand. "Well, you seem to have a very pretty picture in your mind of your St. John, as if he were some Greek god as beautiful as Apollo. And here you are, walking with the monstrously ugly god Vulcan, who is blind and lame besides."

"At times, Edward, you try to be as ugly as Vulcan," I teased.

"And did your St. John come to your school and to your cottage often?" he went on.

"Yes, as he was teaching me the Hindustani language," I replied. "He wanted me to go to India with him."

"He asked you to marry him?"

"Yes, several times," I admitted.

"Then you may leave here immediately," he stated. "It is clear that you love him if you gave him cause to ask you to marry him."

"So push me away, Edward," I said, planting my feet directly in front of him, "for I shall

I Married Him.

not leave on my own. St. John Rivers will never be my husband. He does not love me and I do not love him. He wanted me only as a missionary's wife. I am not happy at his side or even near him, not like I am when I'm with you. Now, do you still want me to go?"

I moved closer to Edward until our faces were almost touching. I saw a smile break across his lips. "Is that the truth, my little Jane?"

"Absolutely, Edward. You don't have to be jealous. I was just teasing you to get you out of your sadness. My heart is yours and will be yours until my dying day."

He kissed me and tears fell from his eyes as he moaned, "Curse these burned eyes! Curse this crippled hand!"

"Oh, Edward, you are still strong. Do not curse yourself. I love only you."

"Enough to be my wife?" he asked.

"Edward, dear Edward, that is my reward. To be your wife will make me the happiest I can ever be," I assured him.

Reader, I married him.

As I am writing this story, I have been Jane Rochester for ten years, wed to the man I love best on earth. Diana and Mary are both married. We visit each other often with our husbands. St. John is still in India. He never married and is still dedicated to his missionary work.

After Edward and I had been married for two years, his eyesight slowly began to return. He had some hint of it when he used to have Mary bring candles on his tray. But it wasn't until one morning when he asked if I had on a gold locket and a pale blue dress that we became more certain he would be able to see again.

We went to London to consult a famous eye doctor who was able to help Edward even further.

And when our first child, a boy, was born, Edward could hold him in his arms and see that his son had inherited his father's strong body and large, shiny, brilliant black eyes.

Edward and I have at last found a life that makes us truly happy.

MAY - 6 2008
21 35

DISCARD